ANOXIC

AARON
SOLOVE

Archway Publishing books may be ordered
through booksellers or by contacting:

Archway Publishing
1663 Liberty Drive
Bloomington, IN 47403
www.archwaypublishing.com
844-669-3957

ISBN: 978-1-6657-0269-0 (sc)
ISBN: 978-1-6657-0267-6 (hc)
ISBN: 978-1-6657-0268-3 (e)

Library of Congress Control Number: 2021902125

Print information available on the last page.

Archway Publishing rev. date: 2/25/2021

1

NATIVE SON

We run, we run, and we run. We keep running until the air in our chests tastes like blood. I smell Mother's milk, sweat, and sunlight. Our hearts beat together as one. The rhythm vibrates in my neck, stretching around to the back of my hair. My eyes water—the salt stings my sight. Mother feels this too. The pain does not stop her. Tall grass touches us, stroking our forms. Long dark hair, cut loose from her braid now, flies wildly in every direction. Behind us, we hear the man shouting. He tells us to come back, to stop running. We cannot stop, never stop. I am weeping with fear. Mother does not cry; she soothes. She says words out loud I do not understand. "This is my child. I do not care its color or origin. This is my child." Mother protects me. What she feels, we both feel. Her strength is weakening. The breath is growing faster. Heat from her mouth washes over my face. The strain is becoming too great. We must stop before we die.

We have finally fallen on our knees. Mother holds me as I rest in her arms. I cannot react other than to cry. She holds me close and tight. She whispers in my ears. I feel her heart beating on my head. The man stands near us. He is so sad. Mother is so sad. Mother stays on her knees. "He is mine. He is mine," she repeats over and over.

The man now sits behind us. He wraps both arms around Mother and me. The man speaks comfort to us both. "He is yours. We will love him always. We must offer him to his real father. The man must be given a chance to meet his son. He knows what he has done. All men must be given a chance to make amends."

Mother sobs quietly, her tears running onto my cheeks. "They cannot take him away from me."

The man responds in kind. "No one will take him. I promise you."

Caw! Caw! echoes from above.

The man points above us to blue sky. A swarming circle of black wings block the light from the sun. The man whispers words to us, his loved ones. "Mother crow has lost her home as we have. She promises we shall survive. She gives us a sign that all will be as it should."

2

THE HOUSE, 1957

The house planned to stand for at least a hundred years. It was still far from that number but had no intentions of going out early. It remembered the men from Dale Construction putting it together plank by plank. They started at seven in the morning every day for a year. Like with the other projects, they had begun by clearing the trees, pulling the rocks, and outlining the property. Every few weeks, different men coming in and out. Some did the banging with wood and nails, others put the shocks of electricity through it. They broke ground and started digging a big hole in the earth. This same group had built the house next to it and the houses across from it. These men groaned all day long about the work. They also laughed a lot and played tricks on one another. It was the young one who they teased. He was the newest and the smallest, so he was naturally a butt of all their shenanigans. The first few weeks were routine, broken up by the men's yelling and laughing.

They stopped laughing after he found what he found in the basement.

It was not a basement yet. But the young one had dug with his spade shovel and hit something hard. He looked down at what it was. When he realized he was looking at a shoulder blade, he called for an older, fatter man.

The man with two chins looked over in the direction of the boy. *What in the hell?* he thought. So far, this entire project had been going smoothly. The old fat man had spent the last twenty years bouncing between contracting companies just hoping for a nice foreman position like this. A large housing development such as this one guaranteed about five years of steady work for him. The laborers were guaranteed absolutely nothing. He had worked long enough in the field to know, if the project did not hit any bumps, his position was secure. In total there would be twenty houses split into four lanes. At the end of each lane was a cul-de-sac—perfect for little Johnny and his sister to play with the other neighborhood kids. Mom and Dad could sip dry martinis while befriending their neighbors.

This was house number four on the block. He was beginning to think four was his new unlucky number. As soon as they broke ground on this lot, things became complicated. Some people had shown up talking about some voodoo nonsense— not even people in his eyes. They were Indian heathens pissed off that their tribes did not have anything left. Not his problem or his people. He called the cops after they showed up for the third day in a row. He had called the real estate managers about what to do if the press showed up. They gave him a hundred bucks to pay off anyone taking pictures. They could take all the pictures they wanted of the finished lots, but the protesters needed to be left out of it. He had pocketed fifty bucks and split the rest between the two photographers for the local news channel. One of the photographers had asked the protesters why they were there. They said some shit about Indian land going back to the Revolutionary War. Apparently the Shawnee had lived on these lands for hundreds of years. The land had been taken from them but remained part of their ancestry. What used to be theirs was now called Pennsylvania. This certainly explained the ridiculous haircuts and jewelry these monsters were wearing. Didn't they have a reservation to pour their sorrows on? Maybe a bottle to drown in? He could not give less of a fuck. This whole development needed to be done, and that was that.

The fat man moved surprisingly quickly toward the boy. He jumped into the hole. Most workers had not been paying attention to the unfolding scene. A booming voice came from down below. The fat man ordered the more seasoned workers down in with him. One by one, they climbed down, afraid their jobs were on the line—until they saw the problem at hand. They argued about what to do.

The youngest of them made the mistake of speaking. "Should we call the police?"

The man with many chins responded loudly enough for the others to hear. "Listen to me, you little shit. You will not mention this to anyone if you want to keep your fucking job. You see that there?" He pointed to the bones sticking above ground. "That is nothing but old dog bones buried here by some punk kid like yourself. Anyone finds out about this, and every man here is out of a job." He looked menacingly at the young one. "I find out you said one word, and I promise to bury you down here with them. Are we fucking clear?" He looked around at the circle of workers to make sure the implication sunk in.

Every man nodded in agreement.

The foreman yelled from the hole, ordering the rest of the workers to leave for the day. When most of the crew was gone, he and the senior workers covered themselves in the hole with a large green tarp. The temperature rose, along with the humidity. Sweat dropped off their faces, soaking through their shirts. With smaller shovels and brushes, they pushed away the dirt surrounding the lone shoulder. The final scene they unearthed was much worse than they had anticipated.

Below them lay the skeleton of an adult in the fetal position. One of them crouched down beside the skeleton. The darkness under the tarp forced them to use flashlights. He flashed his light through the center of the still bones. The man turned to ash. His face dropped, along with his light. The senior fat man, now drenched in perspiration, shoved the stunned worker to the side. The man dry heaved into the dirt. He looked inside at a small pair of black eyeless bones. This man or woman died holding a child. There was also a stench rising from the mud. The smell was something rotten, but it couldn't possibly be from the corpses. These bones had been here for generations, possibly centuries.

These were not timid men, yet they stood shaken. The bones stared the fat man in his face. They backed away once all the bones were completely unearthed. The beams from their flashlights glittered off the eerie relics in the center of this dark, muddy crater. The bones were cracked in places and stained by years of damp earth.

The men did not see the cloud rise from the ground. It moved behind them and under their feet.

"They found us here in the dark, Mother."

"Yes, my child." The cloud circled under the tarp, observing the scene.

"They should let us sleep, Mother."

"We shall teach them, my child."

The fat man stood near the center of the others. His voice was loud and offensive. The cloud moved above him, unnoticed in the dark. The word "sadness" floated from the cloud and vanished onto the fat man.

In the dark, they dug a deeper hole inside the current one. Down they went, foot by foot. The smell must be coming from somewhere else, they decided. Still, they argued about what they were doing. But they never stopped digging. Hours went by, and they dug in the moonlight. The hole was so deep not even the night skylight could reach the bottom. Finally, exhausted and filthy, these men pried the bones apart. They used hammers and crowbars to separate ribs; rip the arms from the torso; and, finally, reach the baby bones in the center.

As a group, they looked upon the miniature skeleton. It lay alone now without the adult wrapping it in safety. One of the burial parties walked forward. Without a word he picked up the child in one piece. He took a last glance at the empty eye sockets and then let it fall down the chasm. It disappeared into the darkness.

When all the bones lay at the bottom, they dumped bags of white powder down on top. They coughed at the acid dust the bags left in the air. They used their shirts to cover their faces, but still it made them choke. They poured thick concrete on top to fill the hole.

The next morning, the work crew from Dale Construction arrived as usual by 7:00 a.m. Every man had driven in silence to the worksite, unsure of what they would find. When they arrived, every man was in shock. The entire basement was lined with concrete. It was perfectly molded, just waiting to dry. The men who'd found the bones were paid in cash.

Construction continued every day for months without

another word of what lay under their feet. They made their way up the floors, the first floor and then the second floor. They put in a fireplace with a chimney. All in all, it was a good house. Sometimes the men complained of a smell. Others made fun of them. If a new member of the work crew showed up, he was warned that sometimes the dog food factory down the road left an odor.

Conversations at the jobsite grew dark. There was fighting between the men. The longer the project, the longer they argued. No one played pranks anymore. Lunchtime became a roundtable discussion of very devilish topics. The men all spoke about the war, who had seen what, and who had been where. They took breaks and smoked their cigarettes while drinking coffee. Some talked about prison, and others just stayed silent. They said the cigarette and coffee masked the lingering odor on the construction site. The foreman stopped eating his big lunches while hurrying them through theirs. One of the workers noticed he sat alone now in his car for most of the day. Some could have sworn they saw him crying. At the end of the week, they would drink beer stashed away in corners of the house.

The finished project was a nice little house. Normally, they would toast such a well-done job. This one time, however, every one of them packed their tools and left in silence. One of them stayed behind. The fat foreman sat by himself on the ground behind his car. The tears came freely in abundance. His eyes bore through the house. His right hand gripped the nickel-plated pistol prized by him at the gun ranges. The crying stopped once his mouth was full of the muzzle.

He looked to the sky, noticing for the first time a horde of crows resting on the finished roof. *Where are all the pretty birds?* he thought.

Then he pulled the trigger.

3

THE VISIT

First it was the older couple who wanted to move further out from the city. Their children were grown already, but they hoped to have a house for the grandchildren. This adorable three-bedroom home was the perfect location. It was only an hour from Philadelphia, with plenty of open space for the grandkids to play freely. It was newly finished, complete with the modern-day needs of a suburban family. Their names were Cindy and Clark. The two of them had been together over thirty years. Together, they had worked as professors at the University of Pennsylvania. Both were scholars of their fields, as well as published authors on American colonialization and African American studies.

Cindy was a particularly respected member of academia. Being a woman, it had taken her years to be accepted into the university. It took her even longer to forge alliances until she was given tenure. Clark was her rock. He had supported her theories and publications even though many found a woman's perspective illegitimate. Career friends had become lifelong spouses.

Both were now semiretired. The new house was meant to be their escape from the city stress. They had a funny way of introducing themselves. "Hi, we're CC," they would say, followed by a simultaneous chuckle.

The couple went to work filling the house with furniture in every room. They liked a lot of color, so the rooms were repainted with yellows and light greens. The two of them had spent years traveling the globe, bringing home all kinds of different ethnic pieces of artwork. They had wooden furniture from India, tapestries from Asia, and rugs from Africa.

They had three grown children, all of whom behaved similarly. Bright candles that gave off flowery odors were placed in nearly every room. Cindy hung dried orange peels from the kitchen ceiling to give it a citrus smell. She had noticed an odd scent that seemed to emanate from the floor but did not bother mentioning it to Clark.

The three adult children came over on the weekends with small children of their own. That first year, the house had become a refuge from the big city. The family loved singing and dancing, filling each room with human delight. The grown kids brought grown friends to their parents' new hideaway. Large meals of varying styles filled the dining room. Afterward, the adults stayed up long hours sipping dark merlot to discuss the ways of the world. Weekends became a celebratory occasion for everyone invited.

On a random Saturday morning, a guest was knocking at the door. No one was expected on that morning. Cindy and Clark had been up a portion of the night drinking with friends on the back porch. It had been Clark's birthday. Both were slightly groggy to respond. Cindy insisted that Clark stay in bed. The house felt the tension rise as she left the bedroom. Her bare feet were cool on the floor. She considered putting on a jacket to cover her nightgown but decided against it. She stopped midstep to look back through the living room.

Three more knocks came from behind her. She could swear that smell from the kitchen was growing worse. There was a cloud of it now all around her. She felt momentarily embarrassed to open the door. With any luck, it was a friendly neighbor they had not met yet bringing coffee and croissants to introduce themselves. She pulled the wooden door inward, noticing for the first time that it was raining outside.

Their guest stood feet from the entranceway. The house knew this man in some way. His aura traveled through every room, every wall, under the concrete foundation, and deep underground. His hair was black, with spots of silver lining. It was held in multiple braids covering his face. He spoke softly to the woman.

Cindy stood at the doorway listening. She did not move an inch. Frozen in place, she absorbed every word. Several minutes went by; only the man spoke in soft whispers. The stranger stepped back off the porch into the rain and left.

"Who was it, honey?" Clark asked from the bedroom.

She stood befuddled, staring off into the storm clouds.

Caw! Caw! Came from the trees.

The woman walked into the kitchen and never answered his question.

4

SHADOW

Movement from above awakens us from restless sleep. We have slept so long together, the two of us. Mother holds me in her arms as she did the day we died. "Shall we travel up, Mother?"

"Yes, my child," she responds.

Up we go through stone and dirt, through the canals of insects, and into the rocky darkness. We see the surrounding. We smell the inhabitants. Mother guides me in a black mist.

"Father," I say.

"Yes, my child. He was here."

Across the halls, into the bedroom we travel. They sleep, the woman and man side by side under a blanket of warmth. "Will they do what is needed?" I ask.

Mother shifts our form through their eyes. Her and I, we read their souls. "Weakness, my child," she whispers.

"I do not want them here, Mother."

In agreement, we pull from their minds and hearts. From

the woman, we take joy. "She will not last long," Mother promises.

From the man, we take sanity. "He will not last long after."

The sun shines upon us. I do not remember such light.

"Remember, child, in the dark, we sleep; we are dead. Here in the light, we are very alive."

The dark cloud leaves the bedroom back to its home in the dry earth.

★★★

It was right after Easter of the second year in the house that Cindy started to not feel well. It had started with her senses. Clark came home from work to find she had lit every candle they had. She had cracked open pieces of fruit. Shards of apples, oranges, and bananas lay everywhere. He asked her what she was doing. She replied through tears that she could no longer smell or taste anything good. There was a pungent odor that was stuck in her nose. The odor was so strong it coated the back of her throat. "I smell something rotten," she cried.

Clark tried to comfort her but to no avail.

"It feels like I can't breathe. Every time I try, all that comes in is that smell."

Clark tried to be understanding. "Cindy, there is no smell. I think you may be delirious. Maybe it's just a fever."

"The dead in the dark are alive in the light," she whispered.

"What did you say?" Clark asked, assuming he'd heard her incorrectly.

"He told me, but I just shut the door. He said those words." She was sobbing so hard it was difficult to understand her.

"Who said what, my love?" Clark asked, now concerned she had begun to hallucinate.

"The man last year. The Indian who came to the door that morning. It was such a strange thing to say. I didn't even have the chance to blow him off. He said that and walked away."

Clark looked at his wife, now more concerned than ever. Clark had always tried to use humor as a response mechanism. "Cindy, darling, I think you mean to say Native American." Clark giggled at his funny politically correct commentary. He hoped she would simply respond with the ordinary don't-be-a-smart-ass glance.

Instead, she wept uncontrollably, looking at the floor. "He told me we would die. We didn't meet their needs." Cindy hobbled forward with her knees bent.

Clark followed her into the next room. She was wearing her long flowery nightgown. Seeing her from this angle, Clark noticed her shoulder blades protruding prominently from her back. His wife had always been a thin woman, but now he was afraid she appeared malnourished. She reminded him of those terrible pictures from labor camps in Germany. They had been plastered across the news for years after the war. He was preparing to talk to her about her dramatic weight loss when they got to the kitchen. Clark found someone else entirely when he turned the corner. The sight took his breath away.

The woman in the kitchen was not his wife. Her eyes were wide. Her hair seemed to have gone gray overnight. Wrinkles had formed cavernous trails on her forehead. It was now he saw yellow eyes that he was certain had not been there that very morning.

"Why did I close the door on him?" Cindy sobbed. She held on to the kitchen counter as though it were a lifeboat.

Clark did not know how to respond. He was sure by looking at her that she was not hallucinating.

"He said they want revenge, but we are not the vessels for it." Then she collapsed onto the floor.

Clark picked her up, carrying her to bed.

She began wailing that night and every night after—so loudly sometimes the house was afraid windows would break. A couple of weeks into the ordeal she began to feel pain all over. The excited light of the family had gone out; in its place was this paralyzed geriatric. She soiled the shiny wood floor with blood and vomit. Clark did not know how to help her. They went to the family physician, who sent them for tests at the hospital. Yes, she was sick. But, no, they could do nothing for her.

Clark had also begun to feel ill. He knew his personality was changing. A deep depression took hold of him. It was not just that the love of his life was so sick. Something was straining his heart. His mood became gloomy all day. Lethargy took the place of energy. Sunlight was a painful reminder of the outside world. The children came to assist but found both Cindy and Clark angry, not wanting their help. Clark locked the doors and nailed the windows shut. He and Cindy lay together on their sky-blue carpet. She cried while he stared at the ceiling, replaying the moments of their lives.

"You're sick, you're sick!" he yelled. "Cindy, what are we doing here on the floor? We must take you to the hospital. Why did I yell at the kids?" He turned her face toward him. She was ashen gray, wrinkled from her thinning hairline down through her neck. Her skin was that of a dying tree.

"We were good, and so we will die." Her dried tongue flecked her lips while she spoke.

Clark released her face from his hands.

"The stranger told me a story." She stared at the ceiling as she spoke. "This was their land. He lived here with his wife.

Our people came one day to take it. They raped his wife. She bore a son that was not one of the tribe's. They brought the baby to the white settlers to show them what they had done. The man responsible denied any wrongdoing. Instead, he and others executed the child right in front of its mother. Although it was not born out of love, she had loved it all the same. The woman swore revenge in her distress. The pain of the loss was too great. She begged her husband to end her life. The man killed his wife and buried her with the baby here on this land. It cursed the earth. They were robbed of their joy. Our people destroyed them. Now they infect us as punishment. They want to wreak havoc on the earth. The child and woman decide who lives and who dies here. Those they allow to live will be their playthings. They will unknowingly seek revenge on all our people. They will be terrors to others and even to themselves." She stopped speaking, turning her head to look at her husband. "Do you smell that? There is something rotten here." Her eyes rolled back in her head.

Only the whites of her eyes were visible. Her chest continued to rise. He listened to her breathing.

Finally, on the third day, she stopped making noise. The house was peaceful again.

The peace only lasted a short while. At night, the man wandered up and down the stairs making soft cries. As he wandered, he would glance at the body of his beloved, now stinking on the floor. Her hair was matted across her face. Her skin looked like dark orange leather. Her eyes were still open. He swore that she watched him as he went insane.

One day, the man stopped getting out of bed. He lay between the sheets all day into the night. The house did not like the body in the living room. It began to leak, staining the wood floors with human liquids. It was very odd. The man had not left the room, and yet the house was certain someone was walking at night. The man seemed too terrified to move. He could swear that Cindy came to see him that night. He continued to stare in anticipation of something.

The man startled the house after so many days of silence. He stood up and walked into the shed in the backyard. The house had always liked the little shed. It was a nice appendage adding to the overall home feelings. The house had been interested to know what the wooded shack had been hiding.

The smell has become overwhelming in the house. A dark cloud hovers over the woman's body. It observes the corpse with gratification. The man sits helpless in bed. The man is of no concern to the shadow. "The woman is gone, Mother. It is the man's turn."

"Yes, my child. He will be gone soon. Do not be afraid. We will rest until others arrive."

"How can we be sure more will come, Mother?"

"Mother crow promised us revenge. Father lives on through the ages to observe the work of our curses. More will come, my child."

The cloud travels away from the rotting carcass on the floor, back to the underground.

The man named Clark comes lumbering back in through the kitchen. He is carrying a metal can. The man lays back into bed. The can is with him; it goes *splish, splosh* all over the down comforter.

The house hears the man make noise for the first time in a long time. He sounds like those construction workers from years past. The man is laughing. First, it is laughter, and then it is wailing, just like the woman. The house feels heat coming from the room. Black smoke chokes the walls. The old man screams until the fire becomes louder than him.

The house wants to scream as well. The best it can do is allow windows to break. The thick burning clouds become alarms for all to see. Neighbors come running with their water and blankets. The house is saved. The man is not. He is found in bed, blackened by fire, with his arms wrapped around the metal can. His ash coats the bedroom floor. They have become mulch in this garden of the dead.

5

FRESH BLOOD

Cindy and Clark's adult children understandably wanted nothing to do with the house. They sold it cheap to a nice couple with two kids, a boy and girl. The realtor had been smart enough to leave out how the prior owners had perished. The year was 1960, and disclosing such events when selling a property was not mandatory. The couple had been searching for over a year for the perfect starter home, and this was it. The realtor informed them there had been a fire on the first floor, but no damage of any kind had been to the structure itself. It was in a perfect location, just north of the city. The house had been given a new paint job in every room. It had started as a light blue but now was a bright white. The outside still had the dark forest green, with black trim along the siding.

The house felt reborn with its new occupants. This husband and wife were like the others on the street. They worked hard together to be doting parents. The father left early for work, and the mother stayed home tending to the house and the children. At night, things were quiet for the most part. Certain nights, they were not.

The house felt everyone moving about. That was no surprise. Much like in the other homes, people moved up and down, made loud noises, dropped things, yelled at each other, argued, and discussed. However, sometimes there were noises later at night—long after everyone had gone to bed. It felt movement through the halls—not all the time, but often enough. It seemed that, when one person started moving, something else would follow. They went in the same directions up and down the stairs. Sometimes they would travel to the basement. A house with movement is nothing new, but it was always strange that there were never any voices.

It went on like this for many seasons. Something was living within it that was not supposed to be. The children began whispering in the dark. The warm couple had become cold to each other. In a short while, what had started as a family now seemed more like strangers sharing meals. The boy and girl had begun spending less and less time together. They seemed complacent to be alone. The boy spoke to himself while crowded in the closet of his room. The house watched him for hours alone in the dark. The young sister likewise created whole worlds with her dolls. Her worlds were not princess fairytales. She created a family with her dolls. This family was very cruel to each other. The older dolls beat the younger dolls mercilessly. The two American Girl dolls gifted to her by her mother ruled the make-believe land. The two odd children populated the upstairs, mostly undisturbed by their mother and father.

The parents, likewise, had become very uneasy. Changes were happening quickly. Every passing month brought a new level of tension into the home. The man would lash out at times. His propensity for violence came without warning. The woman never seemed afraid. She had been a doting mother not long before. Now, she was cold, shut off. She defended the man, disregarding the well-being of her own children. Much like Cindy, who had wailed in pain, the man's screams made the house shake. His scream was primal. Rage engulfed him until there was no longer a father and husband in his soul, simply a beast.

The house watched the several times other men in loud cars with bright colored lights pulled into the street. On many occasions they took the husband away. Days, sometimes weeks would go by before he would return. The court system had forced him to see a doctor to deal with his aggression. When the wife or children asked about his meetings, the man recoiled with hesitation. His anxiety visually amplified before them. After several months of moral deterioration, the husband secluded himself in the basement not to be disturbed. His two children and wife stood outside the basement door listening intently.

For a week, he remained confined. A scratch here, a hammer sound there was all they heard coming from below. "What's he doing down there, Mama?" the boy and girl asked.

"Your father is making renovations on the house." She smiled back at them. In the depths of her stomach, their mother was worried sick.

From the corner of her ears, the little boy responded, "Maybe he should stay down there forever." He followed with a chuckle.

Their mother turned to see her children skip away seemingly almost elated.

Unnoticed by the family, darkness hovers in the corner watching the storm. "The children are behaving well, Mother."

"Yes, my child. Together in the dark, we visited the little ones many moons before. We shall instill selfishness into them. We take empathy away," Mother says.

I wish to have been that age. Life was taken before I had the chance. I am only grateful that Mother and I rest here in the dark. Now we see the children seeking vengeance for us. The boy toys with the adults. The girl remains in his shadow. The father we visited many times. He was already afflicted with fear. Together, Mother and I stain his children. They inspire his nightmares. So scary they have become to him. We travel up into the rooms, listening to him scream. He shall be one of many who we force into the grave.

"Here we are alive, Mother, as you said."

The cloud drifts over the heads of the three and down into the basement, watching the father in the dark. He is covered in filth. Into the wall, he hammers and digs. The father stops what he is doing. He turns now, looking at Mother and me. We look back at him.

"Does he see us, Mother?"

"No. He smells us. He digs, hoping to find us. He is weak like the others before him."

To the dark earth we travel under his feet.

"Let us return to the dead, my child."

"Yes, Mother."

The cloud passes under the father's feet into the concrete floor.

On the third day of her husband's household renovations, the phone rang. It was the psychiatrist assigned to her husband's case. To her surprise, the doctor requested an interview with the children. He had a professional manner over the phone. He brought a calm assuredness that the woman had not felt in a long time. "Your husband seems to be going through what we have diagnosed a manic-depressive state. This can be attributed to his time in the war. We see many soldiers returning with shock-like symptoms. However, he seems to focus on your children during therapy. He says that his kids are not his anymore."

The wife was taken aback at this divulgence.

The doctor explained to her that nightmares were overwhelming her husband. "There is a woman and boy he claims to see that have taken your children away. He is suffering from delusions. The reason I want to talk to your children is to ascertain if there is a way they can support him. If they change their attitudes a bit, maybe it will help." The doctor told her this from his mahogany-stained office in the VA center. He had an upbeat demeanor that gave her hope.

Most doctors she had ever met spoke to her as though she was mentally disabled. This doctor seemed to understand a wife's concern more than others. Greta Volos hung up the phone with a sigh of needed relief. The doctor had a good plan in mind. Maybe the children were the key to alleviating her husband's pain? She listened at the basement door. Clanging and clacking continued below.

Caw! Caw! Startled, she turned around. The noises from the basement ceased. She looked now through the kitchen window over the sink. There, a group of black crows, many in number sat perched, watching her. There was silence now in the basement. Silence in the kitchen. Countless black eyes watched the stillness.

He had seen many cases over the years concerning past traumatic experiences. Dr. Connor McMannis considered himself on the leading edge of psychiatric therapy. He believed, unlike many of his colleagues, that, through therapy and moderate medication, a person could improve his or her life. He felt that his generation suffered the most, stemming from untreated wartime injuries. While the public often only considered a physical injury to be relevant, he felt the emotional injuries could be just as gruesome.

A common theme among all his patients was their reported use of alcohol. In most cases, both wives and other family members had commented on the excessive daily intake of it. These patients were then categorized as "functioning alcoholics"—a general term used by nearly every other doctor he had spoken to. Dr. Connor McMannis had a different idea of it after his own personal tragedy. He looked to his beautifully custom-carved desk resting in the middle of the office. There were carvings of winged angels battling the mighty devil on the sides of it. The top was flat cherry wood. A sheen from the chandelier light came through between space among his paperwork. His attention only brought him to one item though.

In the right-hand corner sat a bronze-encrusted letter opener. The handle was shaped of a lion. The silver dagger was decorated with a well-known symbol. The symbol was of a cross broken in half and redesigned. In the decade prior, it had represented the evil of all humans created by God. Dr. McMannis always made a point of keeping it concealed so that no one would take notice. It in no way represented his own beliefs or ideology. It was a nostalgic memento.

Seventeen years prior, his older brother Fred had returned from the war. He had spent three years tearing through Europe on the hunt for Nazis, like most of the world. Fred was everything to him. He was loud, egotistical, obnoxious— he was everything. On the day Connor and his parents picked Fred up from the naval yard, he'd handed his little brother, Connor, that letter opener. He claimed to have taken it off Adolf Hitler's personal desk. Connor knew, even as a younger man, that his brother was prone to tall tales. It's what made him so endearing to the family. The truth was Connor never cared about the letter opener. He was just so happy to see his brother.

Fred, like so many others, began to drink excessively after he came home. People around Connor who were supposed to be responsible adults wrote it off as men doing what men do. But what if Fred was sick? What if he was not an alcoholic? What if alcohol was the only medicine available to him?

Two years after returning home from killing devils in human form, Fred died. He drank for three days straight before driving his car into a tree. Fred's death took everything from Connor. After some time passed, it gave him a clear goal in life. He was always grateful to his brother for giving purpose back to him. He had garnered more success than most his age. He tried to remain humble. The unspoken truth was that he would give it up to have his brother back.

Dr. McMannis was currently looking at the file of Leonard Volos. The man had been married for fifteen years and had two children. He'd served in the army infantry corps on Okinawa. Okinawa had seen some of the most horrific battles in the Pacific. There was no doubt that Leonard was an excellent specimen for therapy. He had a twelve-year-old son named Michael and a ten-year-old daughter named Mida. According to their mother, the children were normal preadolescent school kids. They did not involve themselves in group activities, but that was no reason to think they are antisocial. The mother was concerned that they were being traumatized by their father's actions. Even in Leonard's own words, he placed some blame on the children for giving him bad thoughts, exacerbating his anxiety.

Dr. McMannis sat back in his plush leather chair to take a moment of reflection. Meeting the children could be a helpful key in understanding why the father was blaming them for horrific fantasies. More than likely, they saw things their own mother was unaware of. Leonard had spoken of the haunting visions he'd been having involving a woman and boy. Was it possible he saw his own children as these scary souls? Why would his mind project the image of terror onto them? Dr. McMannis smiled with curious delight. He spoke out loud to himself. "Oh the mind, you are so damn tricky. You never cease to amaze me." He loved putting together the puzzle pieces of the human brain. The connection of emotion and logic from right and left cortexes that may or may not play out to a person's advantage made his career never ending. The mind would never be fully understood by humanity. He only hoped he could contribute in some small way.

Dr. McMannis snapped back to reality. There was a knock on the office door.

"Hello, children, my name is Dr. McMannis. You can call me Connor. I know your names are Michael and Mida."

The children sat in silence across the row from the doctor. Their mother had told them on the way that their visit was to help their father. Mida had braided pigtails into her hair, giving her a more innocent middle school look. Dr. McMannis wondered if her outfit was genuine, or masked something deeper. Michael wore his hair parted in the middle. He had even splashed on a little of his father's aftershave. They both wore black sweaters with white button shirts underneath. Their mom wanted them dressed as though they would for church.

"Mida, I understand you are ten years old. Is Michael your strong older brother? Does he protect you at school?"

This elicited no response from either child. They sat, staring at the doctor. He felt an urge of anxiety building in his legs.

The children had not even made facial twitches, which struck him as odd.

"As you two know because you live in the same house, your father has not been feeling well. When we treat patients here, we try to pinpoint exactly what is bothering them. The obvious problems associated with your father come from the war. Those are very scary things that even grown men struggle with long after their fighting is over." He paused the speech for a moment to allow these considerations to sink in. It had not occurred to him until just now that he really did not talk to kids that often. These two were quieter than most, so naturally he assumed they may not be the brightest. *Best to continue slowly, Connor,* he said to himself.

"What is a little odd in your father's case is that, for a long time, he seemed OK. Your mother has told me that it really started a couple of years ago, around the time you moved into that nice new house. Do you both like living there?" he asked, this with a smile.

To his relief, the girl answered him, "Yes we do. We've made friends."

The doctor's eyes perked up. "Well, that is wonderful! It's good to find friends at your age. Your father, unfortunately, does not really talk to his friends anymore. Your mother thinks that is contributing to his depression. He says that you guys and your mom take up most of his time—not that he minds it of course. You are, after all, his family and, therefore, his responsibility. He also talks about strange things that may or may not be real—specifically, another woman and a small boy. Has he ever mentioned them to you?"

The children glanced at each other. The girl lowered her head. Michael continued to glare at the physician. The boy then stood up, walking away from the two. Dr. McMannis observed the boy circling around the office. He ran his hands over the plaques adorning the wall, eyeing the books piled high on the shelves.

After waiting several uncomfortable minutes, Dr. McMannis decided to continue. "I think it would help if you guys would try to be a little patient with your father. Think about what it would be like if you did not have friends. He is feeling very alone, and now he is fantasizing about ghosts and silly things like that. Do you guys think you could help him out?"

Michael turned his head sideways, revealing a big smile across his face from the other side of the room. The boy walked back to his chair across from the doctor.

"What I mean is that—"

Michael cut him off. "What you mean is that you do not know what you mean. I am deeply sorry, but you have no place in our life. What happens to our father is our business."

The doctor had been focusing so hard on finding the right way to talk to the children that he had not seen Michael bring the letter opener out of his pocket. The boy moved from the chair to the doctor's feet. He outstretched both arms, placing them firmly on the doctor's knees. His grip was like a vice. Dr. McMannis tried to reach forward, but the boy was too quick. He brought his right hand upward, bringing the dagger to the doctor's Adam's apple. Dr. Connor McMannis's stomach turned over. He could not move.

The little boy spoke in a calm, soft manner. "It is fairly obvious that the people in our house are going through a hard time. We must look out for each other. You can do all you want for others, but please do not bother us again."

Fear was coming at the doctor from multiple angles. His teeth chattered. "I only want to help."

The boy allowed the tip of the letter opener to touch the

man's throat. He twisted the silver blade, forcing the doctor to quiet himself before he might begin screaming.

Mida brought her left hand to Michael's shoulder. The boy bit at his sister in the air. She lowered her head and pulled her hands back into her lap.

"What is wrong with you children?" Dr. McMannis exclaimed. He looked up to the vaulted wood ceiling of his beautiful office. Tears began to form in the corner of both eyes.

"There is nothing wrong with us," the boy said. He came around to the doctor's left side. The blade did not move from his throat. Michael whispered in his ear. "What is dead in the dark is alive in the light. Do you understand what that means, doctor?"

Dr. McMannis looked down his nose. Sweat beaded in his nostrils. He could feel the tip of the letter opener pushing on his skin. It had not gone through yet. Only a little more force would do it. "I don't know what that means," he shakily responded.

Michael put his left thumb in the doctor's mouth. He pushed down on his bottom teeth, forcing his mouth open. The dagger remained in position. "Mother always tells me to stop biting my nails. I have done it all my life. I bite the skin down so far it bleeds around the corners of my fingers. I only do it because everything else is so boring. Pain is never boring, doctor." Michael released the doctor's mouth. He held his left hand in front of the doctor's face to see.

Dr. McMannis took a good look at the small hand. The boy was missing skin around all five nails. Small blood trails traced over his little knuckles.

"I do this to myself for fun, doctor. Think of that the next time you want to be alone with us."

A knock came to the door.

In a second, the two children were back in their seats.

Mrs. Volos stuck her head in. "Sorry to interrupt. We are supposed to be meeting Father for dinner. Doctor, do you mind if I take them?"

Dr. Connor McMannis sat in sweat. Urine soaked through his leather lounge chair. His skin was white.

"Thank you for talking to us, Dr. Connor," Mida said.

The two jumped up and turned to exit with their mother.

Connor looked at the empty chairs, wondering for a moment if that was just a bad dream. He brought his palm to his throat, feeling a small indentation. On the arm of the boy's chair, a silver carved swastika looked back at him, stabbed into the leather.

6

SHINY BADGES

The house remembered the day of crying. It felt loss in years past. Nothing had prepared it for this. The family of four had now been living in the house for three years. It was now 1963. The day prior, both the mother and father had left with the car. They told the children to behave themselves. The mother explained there were things that couples had to work out together. The father had yelled all night long at the shadows on their bedroom wall. He swore the family had cursed him. He felt guilt and betrayal at the same time. This life was no longer his. He despised them all.

From upstairs, his daughter and son heard the man's pleas for freedom. More interesting to them were his rants about shadows following him. He said a foul-mouthed woman yelled into his ear's day and night. When he slept, a small boy with dark wrinkled skin crawled up his legs, biting his knees. An odor lingered on his tongue, stinging his eyeballs. The children listened intently, huddled upstairs. They listened through the vent shaft that went from under Mida's bed directly to the kitchen.

"I know that boy," young Mida said.

Her brother looked at her with a smile on his face. "I know that woman."

It was no surprise that their mother and father needed a day away. The children obeyed their parents, occupying themselves with projects in their bedrooms. The day grew long. The light in the sky began to waver. The house knew the parents had left early. It was now dark outside. The parents had not yet returned. Car noises echoed in the background of the neighborhood. The cars stopped in front of the home on Derry Street.

The little children popped their heads out of their rooms. Together they glanced at the steps leading to the first floor. In the distance came a knock. The knock was followed by several more. It was not a hard knock, rather gentle. The house appreciated the care the visitors took with the door. The children slowly walked down the stairs taking in the growing noise outside. Both brother and sister now stood in front of the door. Two more soft taps came from the other side. The little girl opened the big wooden door. There stood several men in bright blue clothing on the porch. The moonlight sparkled off their metallic badges. They removed their hats and asked the small children to come with them. The children obliged, closing the door behind them.

The house felt very alone that night. Hours ticked by. None of them had come back. The windows had been left open. Cool air in the summer night drifted in, raising and then lowering the curtains of the dining room. Dew from the grass scattered across the yard. It collected in the gutters and puttered down the siding. The house cried softly, wondering where everyone had gone. The rooms remained quiet until the morning. The sun's orange rays came through the windows first. It glittered off the dining room chandelier and bounced into the living room.

The two little children came home that day without parents. They had entered so softly through the front door not even the floorboards were awake to creak at their arrival. The men with loud cars had brought them home. The cars were not loud this morning. The children did not speak as they made their way upstairs.

Other people the house did not recognize began to show up. They wore uniforms and suits, all with badges stapled to their chests. Tension in the house increased by the hour. Something terrible had happened. They took their time with the boy and girl, relaying stories and asking questions. The children remained calm. Their demeanors were noted by the adults. Several of the men began to cry while talking to the children. They seemed sad in a way. The little boy and his sister did not. It was decided that a suitable home was needed for the boy and girl.

Some of these unknowns stayed in the house as monitors. The house was insulted at this. If it could scream, the house would wail at the thought of not being suitable. For days and weeks after, there was silence. The children did not speak to the adults or each other.

When the children seemed to be in the depths of their deepest despair, a stranger showed up on the front porch.

7

A WELCOME STRANGER

Although he was unknown to the children, the stranger was known by the house. A whistle from below drew their attention. The brother and sister saw him from their bedroom windows. He was an older man, with dark. slightly sunburnt skin. He wore a braid of hair both black and silver. He was not a weak-looking man. He stood very still out front. He waited patiently. The children watched, perplexed at the scene. From the front stoop, he turned his face upward directly at them. They saw now he was much older than first appeared. His skin turned like leather. He stared with large dark eyes.

The little sister saw something recognizable in the man. "He has doll's eyes," she said. She lifted the doll in her right hand—a stuffed bunny rabbit she called Mr. Buttersworth. "You see," she said.

The little boy looked at the doll. His sister was right. The doll and the man had the same dark eyes.

The man brought his hand in the air, beckoning them down.

"Should we go?" the boy asked.

With no response from his sister, the boy stood nodding for her to follow. Like soldiers with marching orders, the two backed away from the window, making their way downstairs. The door was already open, although they were sure it had been closed. They stood now in front of the stranger. He leaned down to look at them eye to eye. The children were not afraid of this man. "Your parents are dead," he said. "It was not your father's fault." "The dead in the dark are alive in the light." The brother and sister looked at each other. "You two have heard that in your dreams, haven't you?" the stranger questioned.

"What does it mean?" Mida asked.

"The dead below your feet have found a home in your minds. They were my family, and so now we are family."

Behind him a flock of black feathers swirled as one, making their landing on the front lawn.

The stranger smiled wide from ear to ear.

The little boy responded, "The police are making us leave. They want us to live at stranger's houses."

"Yes," the old Indian said. "But you will find each other among the crowds. You will reign havoc on those who try to replace your parents." The man looked up over the heads of the two children. He spoke aloud. "I can still see them, although they lie beneath our feet. Your people chased us, beat us, and tortured us on our own land. My love went insane. I could not blame her. I buried them here to be at peace. Once again, your people would not allow it. I cannot help you little colonists. I can only watch. Your road has been made with cracks. Your children will be a scourge on your own people. I will see you when you return." The man looked them directly in the eyes before turning to leave.

Little Michael and Mida were left standing hand in hand. The girl held her bunny tightly while it too stared at the exiting visitor. "Should we be scared?' Mida asked.

The man stopped short. He took a moment to observe the dark movement above their heads. "No, little girl, only those around you should be."

The boy smiled wide, placing his arm around his sister's shoulders.

Down the road the old man walked. He'd told the children what he could. The rest they would do on their own. He stopped to look at the house while it was still in his sight. There, in the top window, a small black cloud rested in the corner. "My loves," he said.

We hover in the window, Mother and me. "Father is leaving us. I miss him, Mother."

"Yes, my child, but he will return to see our work. He was right to speak to the children. They must know their home is here. They will bring their own offspring. And so, our justice will thrive." We stay here in the light just a little longer saying goodbye to Father.

The following day, the children were taken by social services away from home. The house, for the first time in its existence, was empty. Leaves gradually collected on its sides and in its pipes. Dust appeared on its boards. The strong concrete that had formed its foundation slowly cracked. The hot and cold seasons came through but still no one entered the front door. Water began to trickle in from small holes in the floor and also the roof. Every day, the house waited and hoped. The silence was deafening.

8

I'VE BEEN MISSING
YOU 1990

First it was a rustle on the sidewalk, a whoosh in the yard, then a *click*. The door opened, and a breath of air not felt in years came in through the front of the house. There were voices, loud voices—two adults just like so many years before. One seemed familiar, but the other was unknown. The two walked slowly through the entranceway. The man clearly knew his way through the place. As they walked, the house began to recognize him. He had grown tall over the many seasons. However, the boy within him remained. The house followed him through the walls. *Where did you go, little boy?* the walls pondered.

The two guests walked from the upstairs, through each bedroom and down into the basement. They peered across the dank underground with flashlights, as the bulbs had long since blown out. The dust whispered in the air, "Who have you brought with you?" The rock walls covered in layers of dirt knew instantly the man had once lived here with this sister.

The boy, who was now a man, guided the woman from room to room.

"Please do not leave again," the boards grumbled.

He stopped at his bedroom where his toys had once been.

The house was delighted. *He remembers us*, it thought. It was suddenly embarrassed at the decay cluttering every inch of it.

After a short while they left through the back door. The house felt afraid that it would be alone once again. A smell from long before seeped up from the basement floor. Several days went by. It began to despair. *Please come back, Michael.*

To its surprise, they returned days later with men just like the ones who had built it all those years before. Slowly, the men scattered throughout the floors. Some covered cracks and removed debris. They even gave the house a new color. The group put things together piece by piece. Sunshine washed through the dank darkness. Workers evaluated and inspected every room—every room except the basement. Michael had made it clear the basement was to be left alone.

On the twelfth night, the two adults came, but they were not alone. They had three little children with them. Once again, the house would hear voices and echoes. *We are so happy*, it thought. Existence was wonderful again, just like it had been.

The years began to tick by. The people—Michael; his wife; and their three children, Christian, Lena, and Natalie—grew older. The house was being used as it was meant to be. Still, it remembered how it was when the people had lived here before. Something was still not quite right. It heard whispers down below. Only the wretched-looking crows would fly across its yard. All the while, there was an unease in the foundation. Michael now was different than the little boy who had left.

What was it about him that was a reminder of the past? It became clearer as time went on. The man was scary like his father. He scolded his children for being afraid. He showed no love nor compassion. At night, there were movements—movement without a voice. Something followed the children in the dark. How could that be? it pondered. For so many years, it had been all alone, with no one to occupy it. But was it alone? Was it ever alone? Familiar fears came through the brick like a hurricane. *Run, children, run far away*, it thought.

"There are three of them, Mother."

"Yes, my child."

Through the dark cracks of earth, the cloud rises from sleep—into the dank basement and up the stairs.

"We have so much time with them, Mother."

"We shall use it, my child."

The darkness moves through the bedrooms at this late hour. It stops at the door of the little boy. There is another dark force already here. "We are not alone, Mother."

"No, my child."

From the ceiling. we watch as the dark figure travels in secret—room to room, playing games on the wee ones. The children cry silently into their pillows, wetting their sheets.

"The children are afraid, Mother, but not of us."

"That is correct, my child. This terror can touch them. We cannot."

"But we can take from them, Mother."

"Yes, my child. We shall take empathy from them. They will grow angry. Together with the dark figure, these little ones will be our revenge on their people."

9

TRICKY OR TREATY

It is always strange going back into the house you grew up in. Fifteen years had passed since she'd left for the West Coast. Things had become complicated after some time. Seeing her family was never a priority. Lena Volos now returned home because her father had finally died. The man had kept on going year after year with what always seemed like no concern. He never wanted to leave the house. Lena tried only once to get him to move. She was never sure why she bothered with it. He was a walking piece of concrete. She was certain he had never listened to anyone in his life. Why did she think he would change later in life?

The siblings had always thought that, once their mom was gone, he would fall apart—with no clue how to function in the world. As it turned out, he functioned fine. It was as if their mother had never existed. They had the strangest relationship, the two of them. It was not until five years ago that he'd been placed in a home for the mentally impaired. Dementia had taken hold of him at an alarming rate. Michael Volos was a monstrous father. A monster is still a monster, even if it is confused.

Her visits to the house occurred very infrequently while living away. The last visit prior to her father being institutionalized was enough. Lena came in the front door, noting right away the smell of rotten garbage. It seemed to get worse the closer she got to the kitchen. The windows and doors had been nailed shut. Lena used the crowbar in the trunk of her new husband's Mercedes to pry the large wooden door open. Not a sound could be heard. She walked slowly, listening intently for any sign of life. Would this be the time she found her father dead on the floor?

Clank! Clank! The sound broke the stillness. It reverberated all around her. *Clank! Clank!* What the hell was that?

"Dad!" she yelled.

Again, the clatter ripped through the rooms. It was coming from underneath her. Lena went to the basement door. "Dad!" The sound stopped. She could hear footsteps crossing in the dark underneath. Up the stairs they proceeded. The sound stopped on the other side of the basement door. Lena heard breathing.

"Why are you here?" came from the opposite side.

With an exhausted sigh, "I am checking on you. You're alone here. For some fucking reason, I actually give a shit."

Silence for several seconds. "I am not alone."

Lena stiffened at this remark.

In a much different, almost female voice came another sound. "What is dead in the dark is alive in the light."

Lena turned white. She felt her blood drop to her knees. She knew that voice but had not heard it since she was a child. Lena backed away from the door, never taking her eyes from it.

She noticed the garbage smell once again. She glanced toward the garbage can, thinking she may vomit into it. Her lips begin to quiver. She was afraid; she was so afraid. It was now that she saw how clean the floor was between her and the basement door. To her right sat the garbage can, empty. The smell was coming from the floor.

The witch's voice came through the air. "Lena."

She was a stone. Bile came from her stomach, sitting in her mouth. With a last hearted effort, she forced her legs into a sprint to the front door. Once outside, she vomited into the brown yard.

Lena had sat in her car for hours after the event. She drove to a mall parking lot far from sight of any customers. She wept loudly, allowing the fear to wash over her like an ice bath. She swore never to return to the house. Hugging herself in the front seat, Lena missed the warmth of all her husbands. She never liked sleeping alone.

Caw! Caw! startled her from the tears. Lena looked straight ahead at a large black crow. Small bits of blood and animal tissue stuck to its bony face. It was joined by another. She looked right and then left. Black wings swarmed around her car. Metal bangs shook her eardrums. The birds landed hard on the roof. *Caw! Caw!* they cried in unison. The screeching grew louder. Her ears felt swollen at the sounds. The noise was overwhelming now. *Caw! Caw! Caw! Caw! Kill! Kill!* The shrieking changed. Lena was sure of it. *Kill! Kill!* The birds pecked at the windows. *Kill! Kill!* Lena started the car. She slammed her foot on the gas, unable to see ahead of her. The engine roared through the empty lot. The birds slowly dissipated. Lena caught her breath. She drove as fast as the engine would allow.

Fuck the house. Michael Volos, her father, could rot there as far as she was concerned.

Several months later, she had received a call from the state police. Her father was found walking down the street covered in gasoline. The neighbors had called it in, concerned the man was clearly confused. The police officer over the phone asked Lena if she would like to meet them at the hospital. Her father had not said a word to them. She told the officer her father was estranged from his children. He asked for another name of kin who could possibly communicate with him. Lena decided against telling her aunt. The officer explained that her father would remain under watch in the psychiatric unit. After seventy-two hours, a relative could come to ask for his release. This all depended on the cooperation of the hospital doctors as well. Lena explained that she understood. However, it could be the hospitals decision as to the fate of her father.

Lena hung up the phone feeling relieved at the situation. She felt no guilt after trying to be a good daughter to a man who never showed an ounce of love toward his children. She received a call a few days later telling her he had been transferred to the Philadelphia state psychiatric hospital for further evaluation. That was the last call she received before his death five years later.

The siblings had been able to tell from a young age that Mom and Dad were always closer than the other kids' parents. To be clear, it was never a loving closeness; it was an oddity— like, if they left each other alone, something terrible would happen. Dad had led the way, and Mom had always followed behind. The children seemed to be an afterthought. Each child individually could recount the zero times the parents engaged them in conversation. The siblings were left to communicate among themselves well into adolescence. Michael Volos and his wife, Victoria, had behaved as if each held off a storm always waiting around the corner. Every person who met their father remembered the man as a rarity. It was a physical impossibility for him to remain still. He was prone to manic rants about nothing that had to do with an active group discussion. The rants were usually followed by a complete downshift in him physically—like a wind-up toy that had run its course.

As he grew older, he also grew quieter. The siblings thought maybe he wanted to disappear into anonymity. He had stopped talking to the very few people he had ever known—not that either of them had had friends to begin with. Their father was never a nice man. And as the years wore on, he behaved like a recluse.

On those rare occasions the children did visit home, it was their mother who did the talking. Talking was an exaggeration. The two of them barely spoke. Their mother would ask generic questions like, How was school? when all of them were no longer in school. She would look confused for a moment until deciding on a comeback question, Well how are the children? Again, no one had children. Visiting them was more of a "check-in." Dad would be somewhere in the house, barely acknowledging anyone's presence. Their mother also got stranger. She got who-is-that-woman-washing-her-car-in-a-storm strange. *Strange* may be a nicer term than *crazy*. She lurked around people. She walked more quietly than normal. Each step was light enough to move over eggshells. When people visited, she seemed to always be semi-hiding in a room. She stopped standing near windows. They were certain that, had she been seen by a professional, their mother would be institutionalized.

On one occasion, their brother Christian had found her in the kitchen. Finding your mom in the kitchen would normally be a run-of-the-mill moment. On this occasion, he'd found her closed in in the pantry. She had been cutting onions for dinner that night. She told Christian that she got the feeling someone was behind her. When he pressed her further, she only retreated further into the depths of the pantry closet. Christian had followed her, irritated at her odd behavior. "What are you doing?" he asked. "Talk to me. Is there something wrong with you?"

Her eyes darted all over him in the dark. She put her hands to her mouth, putting her index finger over her lips. She whispered softly, "I'm scared."

Christian did not move at those words. "What do you have to be so scared of?" He gritted his teeth, seething. "What are you so afraid of?"

His mother's eyes stopped panicking. She looked at him now. "Of them." She covered her face with her hands.

He paused, taking it in. He moved his head forward to question her further. She pushed him directly in the chest, forcing him out of the pantry. She grabbed the handle and shut herself in. Christian stood there. looking at a closed pantry door. He could not believe that inside there was his mother—a grown woman who was supposed to love him, hiding behind a small wooden door.

They had never known her to be a superstitious woman. When they were children, she would berate them for thinking anything was scary in their own home. As adults, they looked back at these moments with only a fraction of the memory. Was she berating? Was she scolding? Maybe she didn't want her kids to be afraid of the dark. But they were.

He turned, jolted backward and onto the floor. His father was standing inches from his back. He'd had no idea he was there. Christian looked up at him from the floor.

"Time for you to go, Christian."

Christian Volos had not hesitated. He'd gotten up and left his parents for good.

As far as Lena knew, that was the last time Christian had seen them. Lena remembered this story Christian had relayed. She sat alone in the dark of her basement. Lena felt very alone now. Her mother was dead, her younger sister was absorbed in her own career, her older brother was completely unattached to reality, and now her father was dead. She would handle her father's funeral and then be done with the family forever.

10

NIGHTY NIGHT

The house was a simple one, with two bedrooms upstairs for the children. The children never minded sleeping close to each other. They were the only group of children on the planet that looked forward to going to bed early. Most kids at school would complain that their parents made them go to their rooms by nine o clock. These odd siblings were happy to gather their things by seven thirty and head upstairs together. It was always safer in numbers. They learned that early on. They were too young to understand the survival tactics that were slowly trickling in. But they seeped in anyway. The children had made peace with the fact that their parents were not going to help them. Together they had to create a code of survival. The rules were as follows: (1) Always use the bathroom before bed. (2) Never turn off the light until everyone was in their room. (3) If you had to get out of bed at night, keep the door open behind you. You never knew if you would have to run back. In the girl's room, Lena's bed was on the right. Natalie's was on the left. Christian slept across the hall. Under his bed was a collection of cooking knives stolen by the three of them from other people's kitchens. The siblings chose to not speak of the strange happenings for fear they would be taken away from each other. The very few stories they heard from their father were about him and his sister being forcibly ripped from their home and placed in foster care. By telling them such stories, their father had instilled a subconscious fear of being separated.

Mother and Father warned the children about the hell that awaited little ones who told lies. What happened at home should stay at home. Their parents had a large bedroom downstairs not far from the front door. Although the house was nearly forty years old, it remained a relatively quiet place. The boards rarely creaked; the doors only once in a blue moon squeaked. It was a steady house with a solid frame. It should have been the perfect family sanctuary.

The kids had heard rumors from neighbors throughout their childhood. The original owners had died due to an unidentified sickness, along with one unsupported story of a fire. After that, they heard bits and pieces of their father's childhood from random "friends." The term "friends" was a stretch at best. Both of their parents were products of the foster system. The only friends they'd obtained were those who shared time with them either in homes or institutions. As the children got older, they realized how much of a mess most of these people had been. Only every other year would someone show up, telling the kids to go find Mom and Dad. They always introduced themselves as aunt or uncle so-and-so. These people were always very thin. Their clothes looked tattered. Very often, they tracked in body odor comparable to rotten fish. The children could remember their mom mopping every inch of the floor after a visit.

Only a few facts existed about their father's life. His parents had died in a car crash when he was around twelve. Their father had a sister who they barely knew. Her name was Mida. Mida had only come to see them once that they were aware of. When they asked about their aunt, the response was always a deflection. The kids had tried one by one to get any information out of their parents. It rarely resulted in a direct answer. All they really knew were the horror stories about Michael and Mida in strangers' care. Victoria, their mother, backed up these accounts.

The three siblings always kept the knives under Christian's bed. It was the only one with a missing wooden board underneath. If Mom happened to snoop around while they were at school, they did not want her to find the knives. Christian's room was the smallest, but it had the largest closet. They always left an extra pillow and blanket in there, just in case something happened in the room. Toward the end of middle school, Lena had developed a system where she would leave a book by the end of her mattress. Eventually she would fall asleep. Inevitably, she'd knock the book off the edge, waking herself up. Once awake, she would crawl underneath and sleep under her own bed. She thought Natalie did not notice. If you shared a room with someone, you tended to notice everything. Christian would sometimes not stay in bed at all. He felt more comfortable hiding in the dark closet with his flashlight.

The horror they dared not tell anyone about was a monster—a real monster. In the dark, the monster stalked them one by one. Their experiences went far and above a fictional creature waiting under the bed. This monster wanted them dead—if not dead, then minimally maimed. Childhood drove them to madness.

11

HOBBIES

Christian carried his notebook wherever he went. In the closet or out, he would constantly be scribbling his comic strips. The fictional comics were made of everything he saw. If he saw a baseball game at the local park, he would begin making a comic series, including every baseball stadium or player that he could think of. When he was younger and watched a cartoon he liked, Christian would make a funny comic of every cartoon character he knew. Similarly, if he were bullied at school, he would keep a running comic of every mean person who came to mind. Christian did not have to be the victim of a disagreeable student to notice fellow students' wrongdoings. Those comic strips were disturbing for such a young boy. He created villains out of the school bullies. The villains in these strips always won the battle. His thought process always saw good deeds as weakness. Christian's comics were outlets; the dark closet and a notebook were his happy place. On paper, the bad guys won. However, in real life, something quite different was unraveling.

Lena created her own type of paper trail storyline. She kept lists of girls in the class who she felt could be the most fun to play with. On her flowery lined notebook paper, she wrote names line by line all the way to the bottom of the page. On the opposite sides were the boys' names. Lena drew arrows connecting names in what became a very intricate Venn diagram. These interconnecting webs would become her little projects on a weekly basis. She would estimate what types of rumors were necessary for which person. She would then decide who the right people were to first hear the rumor. *If Katie thinks that Courtney kissed her boyfriend Nick during the football game who will she attack first?* Lena made bets with herself about how it would play out—the more traumatizing the better. She did not think anyone noticed. Even if teachers did notice, there was no one to tell. Her parents certainly had no interest. On the few occasions she was confronted as an instigator, Lena came prepared to pass the blame onto another student. This allowed the game to continue year after year.

Natalie fell into science fiction and fantasy reading. She could never understand why her sister and brother were so entranced with society. Her books were a much more comforting place to be. She read Jules Vern, JRR Tolkien, Frank Herbert, and so on. These worlds colored her mind with thoughtful reprieve. Natalie suffered from bouts of insomnia, as did her siblings. It was not uncommon to find all three of them in complete silence at three in the morning, plotting out the day or reading about foreign lands hiding wild beasts. While the other two wrestled without sleep, Natalie found it to be a quiet reflective time—the only time of day with no environmental stimulation. It could have been the perfect time, if not intermittently interrupted by the problems lurking in their own house.

The Volos children had to create outlets of war outside their own home. Inside, they continually lost.

12

NIGHT TERRORS

For each of them, the haunting experiences were unique. Sometimes it would happen in the middle of the night. Other times, it was just a quiet afternoon. None of them let their guard down. Natalie was the first to experience it. She had gotten up in the night but came running back to the shared bedroom covered in sweat and panting. Her ankle was bleeding from what looked like a dog bite. They did not have a dog. Natalie had told them that it started as a hiss somewhere in the hallway. The hiss had gradually turned into a voice. It was unlike any voice she had heard before. When her siblings had tried to get more information out of her, she'd finally said that it reminded her of the witch in Snow White. The voice spoke softly but clear enough that she could make it out. It seemed to be all around her. The voice told Natalie she had a funny smell. She swore there was a disgusting giggle—like the witch's mouth was filled with phlegm while speaking to her.

This was the only time Christian and Lena laughed at her. "Maybe if you didn't stink, monsters wouldn't come after you," Christian joked.

Natalie was too terrified to be embarrassed. Dread filled her mind, not only for herself, but also for her siblings. Not long after Natalie's dog bite, the two of them had their own encounters. Christian's was only weeks later, while Lena's occurred the night before Christmas break. In both events, they reported the voice of the Snow White witch.

Collectively, they told each other it could not go on like this forever. They could never have known that this was their new normal.

A walk to use the bathroom in the middle of the night could turn into a fight for their lives. The shadow moved quickly, faster than they ever could react. Not every night but often enough, one of them would experience the dark come alive. An unease settled in their souls. The darkness reached out and grabbed them. The first few months they felt protected with a knife under the bed and an escape route back to a bedroom.

Eventually, things started to happen regardless of their preparations. Lena was the first to find out the bedroom was not a safe zone. She had left her book alongside the bed as she normally did. After a couple of hours of fitful sleep, she rolled over, knocking the book off the edge. She was startled awake not because the book had fallen off, because she never heard it land. She had trained herself to wake up at the sound of the sliding motion it made across the sheets. She woke breathless, waiting for the book to hit the ground. To this day, Lena remembered the feeling of sheer terror in her soul.

She lay still, staring at the ceiling. She spoke to herself, "The book didn't make a noise."

In her right ear came the witch. "I smell you," it said from below the edge of the bed.

Lena began to wet her sweatpants. The bed creaked slightly. Lena turned her head to the right and looked face-to-face at nothing. She strained harder, but the demon had left.

"I saw it."

Lena's eyes darted across the room, and there was Natalie staring back at her.

"No, I see it," Natalie corrected "Don't move."

"Why?" Lena asked.

Natalie pointed to the bedroom door. In the dark, the girls could make out a slight movement. Yellow eyes were blinking at them. The shadow separated from the rest of the room and stepped out into the hall. Their room was still. Both girls took a deep breath, turning their heads to look at each other. From across the hall came a cry. They knew where the witch had gone.

13

DRY YOUR EYES

The house wanted to cry to hard at night. It watched from the ceiling that rotten smell from deep below rise, infesting the children. The smell took the form of a small cloud. This cloud invaded their dreams, warping their minds. It could see their faces being contorted while they slept. It was a good house, a solid house; this was so unfair. The molding on the wall pleaded with the cloud to leave the boy and girls alone. The cloud ignored all, continuing its path into their minds. It stayed away from the parents, for they were its accomplice. Madness was overtaking the little ones. The house was so angry. All it could do was watch—because a house is all it was.

Horrors were countless for their lives. As they moved from grade to grade in school, the children exhibited strange behaviors. Christian never spoke unless ordered to. He spent nearly 100 percent of his time drawing his comic strips. His characters changed every day. He rarely let anyone look at them. His classmates would make sensational outbursts to get a reaction from him, which rarely worked. No one besides the siblings ever knew the stories he created on those pages.

Lena, on the other hand, was a master manipulator. Lena tiptoed between groups of friends, mentioning make-believe rumors. Lena's lies kept her days interesting. She prided herself on the ability to take best friends and turn them to enemies. Teachers complained every year to her parents. Their parents were indifferent to the goings-on of their children. Natalie went out of her way to not be noticed. She took her books to school, left school to complete the assigned homework, and hid away in her room. She did not want friendship from anyone. The teachers, likewise, mentioned this to her parents. From middle school through high school, the parents never once responded to a teacher's concern.

Only on a handful of occasions did the kids bring friends back to the house. Things were usually OK for the first hour. The friends always mentioned an odd odor. Poor Lena made the mistake of befriending a sweet girl named Ginger. Ginger and Lena were inseparable at school.

They enjoyed taunting the boys, playfully flirting with them. Ginger came over on a Wednesday afternoon not long before the girls finished seventh grade. Lena was ecstatic to have a friend at the house.

"Who is this?" her mom asked.

"Mom, this is Ginger, the girl I told you about. We're going to study upstairs for history."

Her mom eyed Ginger up and down, making Ginger extremely uncomfortable.

"Thank you for having me, Mrs. Volos," Ginger said, trying to break the awkwardness.

Lena's mom moved in close to them both. Valerie Volos scanned through them.

"Mom, you are being weird," Lena emphasized.

Her mom stopped her staring, "Am I? I apologize." She left the girls for the kitchen.

The two girls retreated to Lena's room, where they hunkered down to discuss which boy had the cutest hair. The hours ticked by.

"Wow, it's six already," Ginger said. "I should head out."

"OK," Lena exclaimed, having enjoyed her first real visitor.

The girls walked together downstairs. Lena wanted to walk Ginger outside. Ginger turned to face Lena. "I hope this isn't rude."

"What is it?" Lena inquired.

"I noticed a smell in the house. Are you guys sure there isn't a cat or something stuck in the vents?"

Lena was taken back by the question. "Oh sorry, we don't have a cat. I didn't notice anything."

Ginger had a puzzled expression on her face.

"What is it?" Lena asked, now feeling embarrassed.

"I shouldn't have mentioned the smell. I am sorry. But, hey, tell your brother not to spy on us! That is super weird!" Ginger exclaimed with a big smile on her face.

Lena turned and looked back at the house. She muttered the words curiously, more to herself than her friend. "He's not home."

Now Ginger looked a little shaken. Her face became flush with confusion. "Well, who was looking through the keyhole?"

14

HINDSIGHT

Sister Teresa eyed the boy from across the room. He would be finishing the eighth grade soon, and that meant sending him to the public high school. She could see from outside the window he already looked older than the others. His skin complexion had grown paler over the years. She had known the boy since the first grade. He forever had large dark bags under his eyes. She wondered if he had slept eight hours in the last eight years. Members of the faculty had brought concerns to her attention several times. There had not been obvious signs of abuse from what they could tell. He just appeared constantly worn down. His face was perpetually buried in those steno notebooks. His academics or behavior had never once been a problem. How were they expected to address the parents?

She'd imagined the phone call many times over, replaying it in her head. "We are concerned because your son appears to have no problems except that he looks tired." She wondered if they would even let her finish the sentence before hanging up the phone.

The two younger sisters had also been admitted to the school. Both exhibited different traits all together. The sixth grader had a knack for mind games. The nuns had watched it play out during recess time. That seemed to be normal behavior for a young girl—the one difference being the sister never retained friends. Anyone drawn to her would quickly become her next victim. Most of the students had already learned their lessons. Sister Teresa wondered if the sixth grader would have any friends left by the eighth grade—or if she even wanted any.

The youngest of the three was clearly brilliant. She had surpassed her classmates tenfold in every subject. Unbeknownst to her, she had qualified to skip more than one year of school. After a very private meeting with the rest of the staff, they had unanimously decided it would be better not to bring this to the parents' attention. The longer they could keep her under their surveillance, the better. The other teachers felt she was too sensitive for the older grades. Sister Teresa saw something else entirely. The girl was indifferent. She was not autistic, which was a new phenomenon coming out in school psychology. She was just smart and private.

Where were the parents? How could there be three children in the school and the parents not have any involvement? It was just so unusual. As Sister Teresa stood still, peering through the window, she watched the boy make quick stencil movements into his notebook. She peered a little closer. Was he talking to himself? Yes, she thought, they were unusual.

15

ADOLESCENCE

It was no wonder that none of them stayed in the house past age seventeen. Christian ran away at sixteen. The sisters saw him only once each when he made surprise visits to their homes five years later. Lena also left around sixteen, in a dramatic fashion. She met a young stupid boy who would become the first in a line of gullible men enchanted by her. His name was Jared. Poor Jared quit the football team to pursue his newfound dream of becoming an actor in Hollywood. What a coincidence it was that becoming an actress was also Lena's teenage sixteen-year-old girl plan.

They made it all the way to Santa Monica in the Pontiac Jared's older brother had loaned him. Jared had left his family a heartfelt goodbye letter filled with celebratory praises on their parenting. Thanks to them, he could now pursue his goals with utter confidence. Both his parents and siblings sat stunned in their small ranch house at the turn of events. Their son and brother only weeks before, was an outstanding student among his peers. The only ambitions any of them knew of were typical goals of a good-looking, talented young teen. He would be prom king. He would be all state. He would go to college. What was happening? Where was this complete personality shift coming from? What they were unaware of was the devilish muse he had met in fourth period biology. This young woman had power over both mind and body. She was an adorable blond. Her confidence mixed with mysticism was what had drawn him in.

Jared and Lena had met for the first time in secret. He'd driven to the football field under the cover of dark. She was already waiting for him. Jared had wondered how she'd gotten to the field, since he hadn't ever seen her driving a car. He forgot about that when she climbed into the passenger seat. He attempted to create small talk when she put her fingers to his mouth, silencing him. Without a word, she dropped her head into his lap, something he had never experienced. For the next three hours, she played with him, allowing him to have several first experiences. The young boy stood no chance.

Within weeks, she had altered his life. He never considered turning her down at the idea of a road trip to California. The ride all the way had been wonderful. They stayed in motels for less than fifty dollars a night. They drank bankers club vodka that Lena coerced a homeless man into buying for them.

Unfortunately, the sights on the Pacific Coast Highway were too great for Jared. The enchanting journey would get the best of him. He was watching the sunset instead of the road. A Porsche turbo, typical for the roads of Malibu but intimidating to a sixteen-year-old boy, cut them off from the left lane. Jared had no idea the proper reaction was no reaction. The inexperienced driver jerked the wheel to the right from sheer panic. He plowed them into a Vietnamese restaurant on the side of the highway.

Lena still remembered the stupid look on his face. The windshield fell inward, stabbing him in the center of his chest. Fresh spring rolls were scattered around the car. Apparently, they had disturbed a buffet style birthday party. Poor Jared would die. Lena sustained only cuts and bruises. Before the police showed up, she lowered the mirror to examine the damage to her face. Nothing a little time and makeup couldn't take care of. She closed the mirror, glancing to her left. At the end of a long wide shard of glass was Jared. He looked at her, pleading for some semblance of comfort. He coughed blood across her face. He was crying heavily. With every breath, a spurt of deep red blood shot from the center of his chest onto the glass shard. He was gone before the ambulance came wailing up the road.

Lena felt no need to leave California. She decided to start her adulthood a little early. With her newly discovered power over men, Lena could negotiate her way into any situation she wished. As she saw it, this was a man's world. However, men were stupid. With a small smile, an arm caress, they melted into her.

By twenty-one she had lost count of the number of relationships she had destroyed. By twenty-two, she moved onto married men. She found the married ones, especially in a superficial land such as Los Angeles, had money. Their wives stood no chance, even with their seven-day-a-week workouts and costly makeovers. All their men were perverts. She gave them one taste of her twenty-two-year-old self, and they melted. Lena lived to hear the wives break over those late-night phone calls. They would beg and then scream, not sure how to express their untold heartbreak. To Lena, this was mother's milk. The stupid husbands would wink at her on the side. On occasion, they would hold her hand for emotional support. How hard they worked for all they had, only to throw it away like it had never really mattered. Lena could not have been happier.

16

BEDTIME STORIES

Natalie waited all the way to the ripe age of eighteen. In truth, she was a shut-in anyway. Natalie rarely spoke to anyone. She was brilliant on paper but lacked all social confidence. People around her always described her as insecure. She was good with that. The truth was she did not care at all. The lack of confidence was a facade. She wanted nothing to do with anyone. Natalie easily qualified for the premed program at University of Pennsylvania. She chose to be a doctor, not because she cared about people but because she felt satisfaction in their demise. A person's worst day was Natalie's holiday. Since her two siblings had left home, she felt no obligation to her parents. If she was being honest with herself, she knew that her parents, for the most part, had forgotten there was someone else living in the house. They mostly ignored each other. Being ignored was the easy part. She only felt hatred toward her siblings for leaving her alone at night. Although they were now grown, it did not stop the occasional haunting.

Months of complete nightly peace would go by. For a while, Natalie even got herself on a sleeping schedule. It was during one of these blissful nights that she nearly forgot where she was.

It seemed fate wanted to remind her. She awoke to a loud bang outside the window. Natalie's head jerked upward, pulling her from a vivid dream. She stared at the window with her neck strained. She dared not move. Her breathing was slow, rhythmic. Sleep began to claw at her again. She cautiously allowed her eyes to close, lowering herself back into the comfortable sheets. *Tap ... tap ...* tap, on the window again. *Caw! Caw!* The call came from outside. Now she lay in bed with her eyes shut, the valves of her heart blowing open. Her skin crawled with anxiety. Beads of sweat formed on her forehead. She could feel the presence next to her bed. Multiple dark pairs of eyes watched from the cold night sky. The witch was here. Something sharp began to scrape her chin. Natalie would not open her eyes. She recognized the weapon. It was a fingernail. It pushed deeper and deeper into the center of her jawbone. Her skin tore. Natalie felt pressure through her neck. "I smell your blood," the hiss said.

Natalie's eyes locked down. There was no one to call for help. She lay in bed with the dark monster. At this moment, she hated her parents, her siblings, everyone. Tears welled up in the corners of her eye sockets. The nail pulled quickly from her head, releasing a small torrent of blood she felt dribbling down her neckline. Natalie waited for long moments before she opened her eyes in the dark.

A yellow evil stared back at her. Natalie's skin went cold. Blood mixed with sweat on her chin. In a desperate attempt to escape the nightmare, she tried to recount the reactionary process of the parasympathetic nervous system—the fight-or-flight response. The eyes stared back at her, turning wide.

Natalie's breathing was getting away from her. The sweat began to pool below her back. "I want to run. I want to run. I want to run," she chanted. A whimper came from the side of her mouth. Natalie closed her eyes and began to weep. "I'm so alone," she cried softly.

Pain, now in her mouth. Two fingers clutched her tongue with vice strength. Natalie's eyes stayed shut. Her tongue pulled until it could pull no further. She began to fear it would be ripped out. The fingers pulled her tongue right out of her mouth. "Shhhhhhh," went the voice. "I will never let you go," it hissed.

Her tongue released quickly, catching Natalie off guard. She threw herself backward into her pillow. Now she let herself cry loudly in the dark. She was now sure of two things: There was no one to help. And the old Indian had been right to say they were cursed. It was from her hatred now that she began to hate all things human. What had been indifference now felt like acid in her mind. Humanity was the real enemy. There was no way for Natalie to know yet just how much she had in common with her two older siblings.

A mist of black tentacles hung over the door frame watching Natalie cry.

"She is the last of the three children, Mother."

"Yes, my child. That creature does our work for us. This one will leave like the others, ripping life from those she meets."

"This is good, Mother."

"Yes, my child."

17

SPOOKY OOGY

It had been years since Christian had seen friend or family. The more time around them, the stranger things seemed to get. He only felt alone near other peopled. Right now, he just enjoyed the cool dark breeze. Nighttime by the water always calmed him down. His anxiety had been getting the better of him. He might even admit that he missed his sisters. Focusing on the task at hand usually helped him. This part of the evening was always the best time for him to work. It was just dark enough to make joggers nervous but not dark enough that he could not see the fruits of his labor. Most people avoided areas of the city at this time of night. These dark wet corners on the outskirts of an old city. Philadelphia held plenty of these being as old as it was. There was a gurgle in the water that slowly floated past. His plan was to wait until the bubbling had gone downstream, and then he could take off. Until then, he would sit here in the still and be calm. He was not without an audience. Above him in the tree line was a cluster of black crows. Over time, they had become a welcome group. Whenever he enacted a plan, they seemed to know where the best seats were.

Christian had learned several years past about the current down the Schuylkill River. It was forceful enough at this time of year to take a two-hundred-pound object downriver. The current could carry almost anything directly through the city and out to open water in about three hours. He had found the perfect inlet just under the Kelly Street Bridge in the neighboring Manayunk area. Under the bridge was a break in the stone wall. The city had never gotten around to fortifying it. The embankment was still tall enough that it never flooded over. So, no one had complained about it. In the daytime, people sat here to fish and drink from brown paper bags.

He had originally dragged a dead deer he'd confiscated from the turnpike. It was a small buck with a broken neck. Christian had attached a cheap GPS monitor covered in a plastic bag to the unbroken antler. He'd watched the little beacon that night float from Kelly Drive, all the way through Center City, Philadelphia. He'd stopped looking after it had cleared the naval yard. *How ominous*, he thought, *to be floating through a major metropolitan city at night unable to call for help*. He felt pity for the deer—something he had never felt for anything else.

Christian snapped himself to the present. It was important to enjoy the reward of his hard work while he could. Tonight, there was not a strong current. Drowning sounds lingered a little longer than usual—a cough followed by a spit and choke.

In Christian's right hand, he still had the Philips head screwdriver. It was stained on the end with human blood and red and white microscopic vertebrae parts.

The gurgling man's name was Thomas Cotton. Thomas was unaware that someone had been following him for months.

A man had been mimicking his movements without his knowledge. Thomas was known to be a pious man. Tonight, this God-fearing man had seen the devil holding a screwdriver, rather than a pitchfork.

Thomas Cotton had been different before his Bible-thumping transition. As a teenager, Thomas had had an alter ego named Chainsaw McGraw. In fall 1994, Chainsaw had tormented the slower kids at gym class. When the teacher was not looking, he would run up behind the kids and push them to the ground. During their mandatory gym sports, he made a loud buzzing noise while sprinting behind his victims. "*Bzzzzzbzzzzzz*," he would yell and then barrel the unsuspecting weaklings directly into a wall. It went on like this from junior high through high school. Being a nerd in school wasn't hard enough, Thomas made it dangerous.

Thomas never knew he was a famous comic book villain. He had no idea why this was happening to him. Unfortunately for Tom, that did not really matter. He was part of a story, and today the story finally got an ending. Christian could not remember a time when he did not follow his comic storylines. It was better that way. Life without an ongoing story was a life without intrigue.

When he was a kid, he had started a comic after trying chocolate chip cookie dough ice cream for the first time. That was an early plotline—so early on that he barely remembered making it. But he remembered creating Tom's character. Tom had been joined by many others—a lifetime's worth of things to do so that Christian was never bored. He was determined to visit them all. His stories had to have endings. It just so happened that today was Tom's turn.

After leaving work, Tom had gotten into his truck. The figure behind him had jammed a screwdriver between his

C1 and C2 vertebrae. In that moment, Tom had become the weakling. Paralyzed from his face to his toes, all he could do was beg. Now he floated with his face just above the water.

The slow drowning was the only thing on Christian's mind. Every time Tom gasped for air, he sank a little lower into the water of the Schuylkill River. If not for the floaties Christian had put around his arm and waist, Tom's agony would already be over. Christian would have to leave soon. He worked the late shift at the Philadelphia Zoo.

There was not a better place to find entertaining stories about life—tales of animals, birds, and insects and of rude parents who might not ever make it to their child's wedding day. Christian felt the rude were a plague on the earth. Every human needed the same tools for survival. Every human was comprised of the same elements. In other words, humans should be equals. One of the reasons Christian had taken a job at the zoo was the calm atmosphere. In nature, all animals were equal, regardless of sex or color. The only instinct was survival. Christian respected that. Humans had decided on their own that sexuality, wealth, race, and things alike make one better than another. It was his job to rid the world of people who thought too much of themselves. To make another human feel lesser was, in Christian's mind, the greatest evil. Those people would find their way into his notebook. Like several others over the years, Christian had plotted Tom's demise months before. He had fallen into a routine around his own schedule. In the normal world, Christian was never late to work. He never created a scene or spoke against people. Christian was a quiet man, always kind to his coworkers. He never took vacations or called out sick. After he punched out, life was a different story entirely.

Every few months after the demise of a villain, he would

open one of his notebooks that contained a kind of "naughty list." He sat alone in his apartment; closed his eyes; and, without looking, would point to the rows of names. Next to the name was their villainous character name. Whatever name was in front of him when his eyes opened would be his next target.

He had no desire to be exposed. Prison was out of the question. The very idea of being surrounded by people in close quarters made him sick to his core.

Starting the following day, Christian would find the person's address and begin the long task of mapping his next target's every move. It had become frighteningly easy to get a person's information with social media. His method was bold but so much fun. Christian would sit outside coffee shops filled with tight-pant hipsters. He would wait for one of them to take their eyes off their computer for even a second. It worked every time. Eventually, one of the men would have to readjust their top knot. Within an hour of patience, he would make a move from his perch. Before anyone so much as noticed the disturbance, he would grab the laptop and be sprinting down an alley way. The person's information would still be up on the desktop. Christian would use a burner phone to take pictures of all necessary personal information. He could then log in from a separate site to begin hunting his prey.

His first stops were Facebook, Twitter, and Instagram. He could get through the pedigree information under the bewildered coffee shop patron's account in under two minutes. He would then dispose of the laptop and be on his way. Once he acquired the target's place of employment and address, the games could begin. In Christian's apartment was a large collection of wigs, makeup, and female clothing, even lingerie. Over time, he learned disguising yourself was not only necessary; it was also a lot of fun.

Within several weeks, he would know more about his targets than their closest friends. He started with the basics. What was their occupation? Married or single? And so on. It was just a matter of stalking his victims without creating suspicion. It had taken practice over the years to properly track a person. People noticed more than he thought.

Thomas Cotton was married and had a daughter named Lisa. Tom worked in the contracting business after some time in the army. He kept himself in shape and ran a tight ship at home. This all made sense to Christian. The man begged to be taken seriously. He wanted to impress other men so badly. This created his own fateful downfall. He remembered Tom at fifteen. He'd beaten up kids up for fun. He'd once slammed Christian's hand in a locker for no other reason than it made him laugh. How ironic that Tom's current predicament made Christian laugh all the way into work.

What was life without a hint of insanity? Christian did not consider himself a heartless man. When he'd left home, it was to escape the suffocating awkwardness between himself and his parents. They had been strange weak people who had never offered protection to their children. They had played the role of doting adults when necessary in public. Privately, their actions were always selfish. Before moving away, he'd lain in bed trying to recall the number of times he or his sisters had walked around with cuts and bruises from the night before— stalked and beaten their entire lives by a dark horror under their own roof. This had formed him as a man.

Unbeknownst to his siblings, Christian had pleaded multiple times for help. His parents, in turn, had reacted cruelly. They'd reprimanded him, even when shown physical evidence of something terrible. Their mom and dad had told the children their imaginations had gotten the better of them. The only people they had to blame was themselves. In a twisted way of mental degradation, the children began to believe they'd brought this punishment on. They did not deserve peace. Nor would they ever have it. From the moment they were born, they had become burdens. Because of that, this living nightmare was their deserved punishment. It was not until Christian grew older that he realized how much he hated his parents for their uselessness. He cared deeply about his siblings and what they had gone through together. It was because of those experiences that he knew they could handle themselves without his presence.

Natalie had reached out that week to let Christian know their dad had died. Reaching out to Christian meant leaving a message with his boss at the zoo. Natalie was always sweet, in a way unlike him and Lena. It did not really bother him that their father was gone. To be perfectly honest, it was kind of a relief. Their mother had always been weird. She'd gotten stranger in her last days. He'd only gone to see them once in the old house. She had kept holding onto the wall like it was about to come down on her. She had barely responded to Christian's questions. Michael Volos, his father, had just watched her and walked through the house aimlessly. It seemed to him that they were both waiting for something. Going back there had only stirred up thoughts of the past—the kind that most adults put into a certain part of their brain and only open at specific moments. He had made a nostalgic stop at the closet. The closet had been his fortress of solitude. However, he'd never felt like Superman. It was just a door against the dark monsters. They never slept. No one ever slept.

After Lena's first encounter when they were so little, the terrors had occurred more and more frequently. He really did hope that both Lena and Natalie had blocked most of it out. For a year or so, he had tried to sleep through the nights, staying in bed. He found himself wide awake usually before 2:00 a.m., staring at the ceiling. His mind danced with all kinds of late-night thoughts. Insecurities he did not realize he had would weigh on him. Memories of the shadow coming for him at night danced in his vision.

He had not seen it, only heard something like a whisper in his ear. He told himself it was just part of the mind games. His eyes had blinked in the dark for only a second. When they opened, there was another pair of wider, brighter eyes staring back at him. They were white with a yellow tinge. A hand latched onto the lower half of his jaw, prying his mouth apart. The eyes came closer in the dark; the whisper became a sound. "I smell you," it said. His fear gave way to utter desperation.

Christian began to weep and scream. Where were his parents? Why was he so alone?

"Sleep," it said, and a hard slap across his face took him completely off guard.

His head had been hit so hard it felt held down by concrete to his sheets. Christian rounded his head from the right. When he looked forward, the shadow was gone. After that night, he rarely spent anytime outside of the closet. Things did not improve from there.

Very quickly he learned there was no safe place in his own home. The part of the house he could never go back to was the basement. Basements were always scary for children, sometimes even adults. What he knew that most adults did not know was that their basement fears were born out of reality. In the basement was an old workbench. Under the bench, Christian liked to keep his notebooks and pens for safekeeping. At some point, there was mention of a fire in the house years ago. Christian figured the basement was the only fireproof place for his treasures. He only went down there a handful of times at night. He was nine the first time it happened.

The house was relatively quiet that night, but he could not sleep. He had not grabbed an extra notebook to write with before bed. Why he needed to go down there, he would never understand. He slowly went to the first floor and through the kitchen to the basement door. Christian could still remember that gut feeling he had opening the door. The musty, concrete smell hit his nose and spread across his face. From the kitchen landing, he went down the stairs with his hand high in the air to catch the chain attached to the lone light bulb. With this light on, he was free to roam to the back where the workbench sat.

That was when the light went out. The door at the top of the steps slammed shut. He'd had just enough time to step next to the workbench when everything went dark. He stood in place, trying to slow his heart to a mere putter. A sound like a thump was continuous in the dank room. Somewhere in the dark was another heartbeat. He dared not breathe too hard or run. Softly, he crouched down to his knees and pulled himself onto the dusty floor and under the workbench. He lay there in the dark. The concrete was cold, but he had already sweat through his shirt.

A shadow moved on his right. There it was in his ear. A soft voice that somehow echoed throughout the entire room. "You have a funny smell," it said from everywhere.

Why was it so dark? He strained to see only a little; it just hurt his eyes with effort. Then the teeth came down on his cheek. He did not move. He froze in shock. The teeth felt sharp and strong. Maybe just one bite, and it would disappear. It chomped down, and he felt his skin break just below his right eye. Both eyes watered; he dared not make a sound. The pain traveled to his eyes. He could tell the skin was already bleeding.

He turned his eyes to see the demon. Turning his head would tear off skin under the eye. His cheek stayed in its bite. Deeper it squeezed; more blood ran down onto his neck. In his ears, all he could hear was his own heartbeat cycling out of control. He looked again. To his horror, he found a pair of eyes staring right back at him. He thought maybe those were eyebrows above them, but it was impossible to tell in the dark. These eyes had a look of pure satisfaction, wide and bright just like before. He held firm, making no sound, even though he wanted to scream. It let go of him as quickly as it had appeared. He heard nothing except the thumping in his own chest. A long, exhaled breath rolled through his nose, filled with dust from the floor.

"The boy is hiding, Mother."

"Yes, my child. He hides in the dark. He does not know that is where fear lives. Look at the monster stalk him as small prey. What wonderful work it does for us."

Mother and I feel the cool mist of the underground. We watch from above as the boy whimpers.

"He cannot escape, Mother."

"No, my child. None of them will."

Christian stayed under the workbench for what seemed to be hours. He gripped the legs of the table, feeling some satisfaction in their stability. He could tell in the dark that his hands left sweaty fingerprints on the dirty wooden table legs. The bench and he were in it together. It made him feel less alone. Slowly, he shifted himself out from under the workbench. He stood in the dark. Christian took a step forward, feeling air behind him. He turned to the dark concrete wall.

There in the dark, was a shape. The shape did not move, but he got the feeling it was looking at him. "It's dark down here," he told himself. "There is nothing there," he told himself. He repeated those words, hoping it was all a bad dream. Silence was between him and the wall.

After several minutes, he stepped backward, turning to go up the steps. That night he let the blood dry on his cheeks. In the morning, he showed Lena and Natalie. They looked at each other with the same thoughts, not needing to say them. They were in this together. Christian went into the bathroom after showing off his injuries. He turned the light off and sat in the dark. He put his hand to the cuts on his face. The pain came back, forcing tears in both eyes.

"It's not a dream," he said alone in the dark.

Several weeks later, while sitting in class at school, Christian's teacher Ms. Gabriel was going through the order of events in the Crucible. She was outlining the dramatic punishments the lead character had to endure simply because she was a woman. Christian had a twinge of guilt for complaining to his sisters about the horrors he was enduring. They were facing the same evil, but for them, it seemed, life would be much more difficult. Christian knew, if he survived, his life would be significantly easier as a white man in America. His sisters, however, would have to fight every inch for their place in society.

Something else hit him at this very moment—the order of events in the basement. Why had the light bulb gone out before the upstairs door had closed? If something had been following him, it made more sense that the door would be closed first.

It's probably nothing, he thought as Ms. Gabriel read on.

18

DADDY DEAREST

Only once in all their years at the house did the children decide collectively to broach the issue with their parents. Christian and Lena took the lead, with plans to tell them straightforwardly what they had been experiencing and to ask if their parents could help them in any way. The two formidable siblings marched into the dimly lit living room with Natalie trailing behind. The old clock, supposedly given after the death of a distant uncle, stood in the background of the wooded room. All three children saw the clock as a kind of timer. In a short while, they would either have parental support or be laughed away. They had not prepared themselves for the response they received.

Christian began, immediately stumbling over his words. "Dad, we need to speak to you about something we have been experiencing in the house. I am not sure how to have this conversation, but we think it is really important."

Their father continued to play with the TV antenna that

sat on top of their black-and-white. The TV never worked. Michael Volos would swear someone was talking to them from the antenna. He continued to arrange the antenna in different directions for a clear signal. The three children noticed, perhaps for the first time, the TV was not even turned on.

Lena, annoyed at the situation, assumed a more forceful approach. "Stop messing with the fucking antenna, old man!" she yelled commandingly. "We have something to talk to you and Mom about. We're tired of not sleeping and being scared all the time. You both know something is not right here. Turn the fuck around!"

It was now their father stopped moving. He remained in a crouched position with his back toward them. Slowly and steadily, his body turned to the left, bending into an unnatural position from his torso. He peered at them. For a split second, they thought a stranger was in the house. Natalie noticed creasing in his left cheek from a thin smile. His body took on a thinner almost sickly form. Without turning completely, he responded. "Are you scared, children? What is bothering you in this old house of ours? I have an idea. How about we go right now and grab your mother. We will pack our things and get out of here to start fresh. Would that help?"

The children stood motionless; his tone said none of those things. His arms raised up on either side. His hands still dangled lifeless. Natalie thought the pose reminded her of Jesus on the cross.

"You are guests here in the house where I grew up. Your aunt as well. Our parents lived here with us. This is not your home. Life is a challenging occasion. It is filled with several pieces of boredom, excitement, and fear. You should pray that your lives contain more of the first two. If you find that boredom or excitement do not meet your needs, then come have another conversation with me. You will find no solidarity here."

The trio backed away from their father. His words cut deep through their souls. Their utter loneliness was now more prominent than ever before. The weight of the situation fell on them like hot lead. As they began their procession out of the room, he told them one more thing.

"Tomorrow we will go visit an old friend. Your aunt and I knew him as a child. Be ready by nine."

In the uppermost corner of the room, a dark cloud watched the father fiddle with the television antenna.

"The children are scared, Mother."

"Yes, my child. Their fear will turn to hate. Hate will project onto the other colonists they meet. The love they seek is not theirs to have."

The cloud watched the children leave the room crestfallen. They slowly walked upstairs in silence.

At nine o'clock the next morning, the three little ducklings filed out of the house with their father. If asked later in life, each of them would be able recall this meeting in graphic detail. So rarely were they able to meet a new person—especially someone who their father and aunt knew. The rain came down heavy, adding drama to the day. Natalie and Lena put on their yellow rain jackets, while Christian donned a sweater, allowing the water to cool him down.

Their father waited patiently in the green Buick LeSabre. The car was the only one they had known the family to have. Every day their father left for work with a trail of exhaust smoke hovering over the driveway. What kind of work he did, they had no idea. He eyed them from behind the steering wheel. Heavy exhaust fumes mixed with humidity in the air. They piled in the back seat, with Natalie taking the middle.

Their father put on the radio to an old-time station. The sound quality was broken; the instruments were crackling. Lena thought it reminded her of jazz she had listened to on occasion. An old woman sang a deep hearty tune describing something about a devil in the details. Her voice broke some of the tension in the air.

The car backed out the driveway, turning right down Derry Street. As the car chugged along the pot-filled road, Natalie took note of a long line in the rain—dark-eyed crows in aisle form on either side of the street. *Are they looking at us?* Natalie thought.

They drove for the last twenty minutes down long pine tree-covered neighborhoods. Whoever this friend of their fathers was, he must be wealthy, they thought. Neither their father nor the three of them had said a word as he drove. They passed mansion after mansion of all colors. Each had wraparound driveways leading to manicured bushes. The front of most had marble columns holding multibedroom estates. The children had never known their father to have rich friends. Gardeners walked along the paths, tending to different parts of spectacular lawn. Dogs ran freely in some. The cars glistened, even in stormy weather having recently been waxed. This friend must have done well for themselves.

Eventually, there was a break in the neighborhood. A lush green field with stone statues appeared on the right. The field stopped on a perfectly mowed line. On the other side, all vegetation sat dead. High yellow grass sagged under the drizzle. Several hundred yards back stood a massive home. It was similar to the rest, with marble carvings and a quarter-mile driveway. Their green station wagon turned into it. The gravel crunched underneath the wheels. They came to a stop out front. No other cars were there. What a funny site, the children thought—their rustic family car out front of this castle.

The children followed their father's lead and exited the car. Simultaneously, they noticed the change up close. The house was in complete disrepair. The stone was stained a thick brown across the entire facade. The foundation was cracked under the entrance steps. What they'd originally thought to be ivy was actually a mix of moss and weeds circling the sides. The numerous windows were nearly all broken. The wooden door had a golden knocker in the shape of a lion. Natalie pulled at her siblings clothes. She motioned forward. They realized the door was left open. The doorjamb had broken beams attached to it. From this angle, the house looked abandoned.

Their father went first—pushing the door open without any attempt at a knock. They followed him, unsure of what else to do. The first thing Christian noticed were the leaves. Brown rotting leaves covered the entire foyer floor. Their father stood in the center encircled by near complete darkness. Something moved in the corner.

A haggard-looking man came from the shadows. His gray hair fell from the sides, but he was bald in the center. His skin was wrinkled and covered in what looked like sores. He ran to their father and hugged him around his torso. Their father made no movement. From under his arm, the man's face peered at the children. His teeth shown yellow. "Michael, Michael, you've brought the children!" The man was ecstatic. He leapt from under their father toward them. "Look at them. Look at you!" He stood in front of the three. He stood over six foot up close. They could tell right away the man was delayed in some fashion.

From behind the excited man's back, their father spoke. "Where is he John?"

"I've left him in the study so that he may study!" He giggled at the joke.

Their father walked to the left of a large set of stairs with furniture blocking the majority of it. Christian noticed large cobwebs dancing across the entrance of the upstairs.

The giddy stranger waved them on with his wrinkled hands. He called from behind them, "He'll be so excited to see you!"

Michael walked in the dark with his children trailing behind. He pushed on a large oak door. An ocean of books lined the walls. The three children took in such a site. There were so many that the colors created a hologram image on the walls. All three wanted nothing more than to run to the shelves and pour over each and every one. Natalie felt almost emotional at what she was seeing. Never had any of them seen such a collection outside maybe a library. What a wonderful place this was, they thought. Christian looked at his sisters with awe. They returned the look of complete infatuation. Their eyes started from the right, tracking to the left.

In the far corner was a different figure. It was a person in a chair. The person was in a wheelchair to be exact. Their father stood in front of it looking down. He seemed not to notice the vast collection around them. The children walked over the carpeted floor. Their father was whispering to the man. The man seemed to shake in his chair. Michael Volos spoke to his children but never looked in their direction. "This is Connor, children. He is a very good doctor. He took care of me and your aunt Mida when we were your age."

The man continued to shake. He was extremely old. The physical state he was in made exact age difficult to determine. Lena guessed he was at least in his late eighties. It was hard to tell if he was shaking due to the cold draft or if his age made him do that.

"Thanks to Connor and all his work, your aunt and I were sent to kind, loving foster homes. There we made best friends—friends like John out there who takes care of you. Isn't that right, Connor?"

The old doctor continued to shake up and down.

"I'll leave the four of you to get acquainted." With that, their father walked to the door.

The children stood alone now with the man in the wheelchair.

"Where the fuck are we?" Lena asked the group.

Both Christian and Natalie ignored her question, taking another look around their current surroundings. "Have you guys noticed most of these books?" Natalie asked.

The two older siblings looked at her.

"They are almost entirely on psychology or medicine."

Now the two took a closer look; she was right. Nearly every book in the massive library was on child and family psychology.

A hand grabbed Lena. She shrieked at the surprise. The old shaking man stared at them. His glasses fell partly off his face. His beard was splotchy with small bruises around the white hairs. The man mumbled. Lena could smell his breath from two feet away. "Mum," he said.

Christian put his hands on the man's wheelchair. "What are you saying? Are these your books?"

The man tried again, "Mum."

The three held puzzled faces.

"Is he confused?" Natalie asked.

"Mum, mum, mum," he repeated.

Christian responded, "I think so. Let us not get him worked up. He might think you're his mom."

Lena asked a general question. "Does he really know Mida?"

The old man bucked back and forth wildly in the chair. Light cracking could be heard from part of its structure.

With a head nod from Christian they walked toward the door leading out.

Behind them the man continued his rant. "Mum, mum, mum, mum," his voice growing louder at every utterance of the words.

"I don't know what to do for him," a desperate Natalie said.

A thunderous cry came behind them. "Run!"

The children stopped in their tracks. They turned to the man in the corner. He sat, now weeping into his chair.

Once again, there was complete silence on the ride home. The only sounds came from raindrops clapping off the windows and roof. In the old steel car, every sound amplified. Each of the children considered what they had just seen. An old friend of their father's was taking care of a man who used to be an expert in his field. With the house and library collection, it was safe to assume he had been a renowned psychiatrist of some kind. They had never been close with their aunt. She tended to be a disturbing presence, similar to their own parents. Their parents could be cruel. Mida always struck them as odd. Now, the three of them felt pity for her. She had grown up in the same horrific foster homes as their parents. She had probably felt as alone as they did. Maybe this creature that stalked them had stalked her as well. Without saying it, they knew their father had provided no support for her. He didn't care about his own children. Why should he care about his sister? Poor Mida; at least they had each other. She had grown up haunted and alone.

19

PITY THE FOOLS

It was her fourth shift in a row. Right now, Natalie was trying to figure out what career she could move into without completely undoing the last decade. She had worked so hard to get through the premed program at Penn. After college was medical school, and then there was residency in Montana. So why was she not happier now as an attending physician? All the night shifts and holidays for what? These stupid patients kept showing back up for the same issues they had been treated for a thousand times over. Eighty-hour work weeks with no breaks, and this was so supposed to be a glamorous, respected job.

Mr. Cadigan, who was in room five, was back for the fourth time this month. There were so many Mr. Cadigans in the health care world. Natalie had warned him and his family that they needed to stay on top of his medication schedule. Per the usual, they didn't listen. They just wanted to blame the doctors and staff so they could sue the hospital for malpractice. His family was like so many others, giving all the glory to God.

"Pray harder for his saving grace," they would say. Her mind would scream through gray matter and skull, *God wants this person dead, you small-minded fools. Do you understand how much the people in this place have worked to create miracles?*

It was always a conundrum to her how people could devote themselves to two thousand-year-old writings by bored farmers in the Middle East. She had always noticed that religious writings clearly worked in the man's favor. And yet, the whole point was supposed to be everyone is created by and beholden to an infallible being. The being created all inhabitants of the universe. For some reason according to all the sacred religious guidelines, certain creatures were greater than others. Wasn't that a huge plot hole? She had taught herself years before that people hung onto those words only out of fear of death. Natalie's belief was that life was nothing but delusional moments of control, right until the moment the plane engines failed. The thought reverberated in her head day and night.

She stood outside the room admiring their collective stupidity. Mr. Cadigan had been a military man, so therefore his family seemed to equate his service to immortality. She had explained time and time again how bad the cancer diagnosis was. They were all in there right now waiting to berate any clinician who walked by. Natalie smiled for a moment, just enjoying what was about to come.

It wasn't her fault that this society prolonged everyone's life, assuming it was all worth living for. She was a firm believer that all surgical operations should be withheld at seventy-five. Not only that, after eighty, no one should receive any type of life-saving medical treatment. The only thing geriatrics would be entitled to was pain medication. She had seen far too many senior citizens go out in agony after such a long life. The least they deserved was a vein full of morphine. Natalie had written her thesis in medical school about the benefits of physician-assisted suicide. Had she not been a brilliant student, the board threatened to keep her from graduating. Fortunately, she was brilliant. She graduated and was given her medical license after rewriting her thesis about the benefits of appropriate palliative care.

What a joke, she thought, typing away with only forty-eight hours to finish the entire thing. People needed to learn to let go. All life was not worth fighting for. The majority of people who died in this world should be celebrated, not mourned. Why did we cry after a person has fulfilled his or her purpose?

Tragedies were a different situation all together. This man was the perfect example of a life well lived and now a death foolishly postponed. Natalie had just finished giving the family the same lecture she had given them every time prior. While she spoke, she looked over the hanging medication bags and IV pumps—writing things down as she circled them in the room doing her very best to look interested and smart. Natalie decided she had had enough of this family. She had daydreams of pissing across the room to mark her territory, scaring them off. They never even noticed the syringe she brought out and injected into a half-empty bag of saline.

A statement made in medical school stayed with her. "Never Push Potassium." Natalie had forgotten a lot over the years, just because of the fire hose of information that was shoved down her throat. She never forgot that. While she was falsely placating to the unrelenting family members, their father's heart was doing backflips. The potassium was creating an arrhythmia that not even the greatest cardiac surgeons would be able to pull him out of.

Not two minutes after she left the room, code pagers started going off across the halls. An automated overhead announcement came through the entire hospital building. "Code Blue, ICU Room 8."

A short wave of panic went throughout the staff but was quickly followed by efficient, professional movements. Which son was that screaming from the room? she wondered. A nurse came sprinting past her with the code cart.

One of the doctors called to Natalie, "Call anesthesia. This guy can't breathe."

Natalie cracked a small smile while she slowly reached for her phone. She remembered why she loved this job.

20

POUR PIGGY A DRINK

Most detectives with the Philadelphia Police Department began with a hard-driving work ethic and a background of gun ranges and gym memberships. Now entering his twenty-second year, Frank was a different stereotype. He liked the coffee at Broad Street Diner. Plus, their carrot cake was just unbelievable. He still went for a jog now and again. But in no way was the man of peak condition from even ten years ago. Truth be told, he just really did not care. If he chased a suspect now, there was a solid chance of getting shot. And if he shot the suspect, not only would he be out of a job, he might also wind up in jail. *No thank you*, he thought. It wasn't that he was waiting to retire; he still liked the job. He simply did not care as much. Police work was much like that of the nurses he worked with in the hospitals. Shitty people came in wanting you to fix their problems. After you'd done your best, they left. And more shitty people were waiting at the door. It always reminded him of waiting tables without the cash tip.

The truth was that Frank could go through the next few years just running the gambit of investigation after investigation. It still excited him, which was more than most people could say in a lifetime. He figured sixty would be his time to call it. The only thing was this stupid nagging feeling in his head. Every time he opened a certain folder, his stomach turned. For over ten years, there had been random bodies popping up around the city. Bodies showing up in a major metropolitan city was nothing new in law enforcement. He had known one of the victims briefly, and that was enough to pull him in. Had it been found out by his supervisors at any time, he would be investigated by internal affairs. At first, he had involved himself to make sure there was no connection made by the assigned detectives. There was no pattern, no motive, not one clear connection that anyone could put together. The only possible resemblance was the violence. All the victims over this long stretch had had something abhorrent done to them. He had been around long enough to know that, if you wanted someone dead, go to Walmart, buy a shotgun, and they are dead. What had been done to the people in this folder was a personal death. All the victims had been killed in a creative way. Frank was never one for coincidence.

In 2002, he signed his final divorce papers. After leaving his lawyer's office, he made the decision to drink until he was kicked out of every bar in the city. His first stop was Monks Café downtown. The sign said café, but the establishment was known for top-shelf bourbon and local brews, all of which suited his needs. It was the perfect environment for day drinking. It was a blustery Friday with overcast skies and nothing interesting going on. He walked into Monks at three in the afternoon. Frank remembered the entire scene up until around nine o'clock. The bar was empty except for a loner in a suit all the way at the end of the brass railing. The bartender was running the glasses through the wash sink and then hand drying them. Frank sat down, already feeling at home. He ordered a double bourbon on the rocks and opened a tab. The bearded bartender was all too happy to comply. Frank sat for an hour, sipping his drink, which had turned into three. He remembered his breathing was slightly more laborious, and he had the overwhelming desire for a cigarette.

The stranger at the end of the bar seemed to read his mind. "You need some fresh air?" the man had asked.

"Probably not the worst idea," Frank replied.

The stranger motioned Frank to head outside as he pulled out a pack of Marlboro lights. The rain was coming down in sprinkles but nothing too heavy to spoil the moment. The stranger handed Frank a butt and offered him a light. Frank noticed the man was probably late thirties, strongly built, but had a stressed look about him.

"Thanks for the cancer. It's exactly what I needed," Frank said jokingly.

Not much was happening in the street around the two men. A cab parked on the corner waited for a ride. A woman with long red hair walked on the other side of the street. Frank noticed her thick muscular legs through fitted jeans. He wished he could run over and get a glimpse of her face under that hair. The body odor from a homeless man wafted in the air from half a block away.

The generous man took a long look at Frank. "You're a cop?" he asked.

"How'd you know that?" Frank replied with an air of suspicion.

The man glanced down to Frank's waist. He had forgotten that his badge was still holstered to his belt.

Frank giggled. "Man, I must've needed a drink more than I fucking realized." Frank was getting the impression that the man was hitting on him. "Look, man, I don't want to be rude, but I don't roll that way."

The man laughed and coughed on his smoke. "Wow, I need to relax if that's the vibe I'm giving off." The well-built stranger flicked his cigarette into the alley. "Actually, I could use some cop advice if you got a minute. I'll buy the next round."

There was absolutely no way Frank was going to turn down this offer.

Together, now as an unwritten duo of destruction, they sat at the bar to exchange slurry stories. The bartender started them off with a double of Maker's Mark and strict instructions to keep them pouring.

"All right, let's have it. Did you get yourself into some trouble?" Frank asked his new best friend.

The man laughed at the remark. "No, in fact, I think it's my head messing with me."

Frank took on a confused look, hiding it behind a glass of brown greatness.

The man took a deep breath. "I think someone has been watching me. I'm not sure, but it's been freaking me out. I haven't mentioned it to my wife because how the hell am I supposed to?"

Frank took a more serious look at the man. He could see the original stressful anxiety he had noticed was accurate. The man wasn't kidding. "OK, well, first off, is there any reason you can think of that someone would want to follow you? I assume you're a regular kind of guy, but I just met you. Don't answer this because it'll ruin both our nights, but are you involved in anything sketchy? Drugs?"

The man scoffed at the idea. "No. In fact, I wish I used more drugs because maybe it would help me relax."

Frank was now more interested in the mystery. "Let's start simple. Why do you think someone is following you?"

At this, the man became white. The color drained completely out of his face. Frank put his glass down.

"Hey, you all right?" he asked.

The man began to shake. With his right hand, he grabbed Frank's shoulder. The man moved in closer. "I know it, because I've seen him." He let go of Frank. In a whisper, "I've seen him. But I don't think he knows it."

Frank turned his body so that he faced the man in his barstool. "How do you know it's a man?"

Another scoff. "The way he moved, his size; I can tell. The first time I was in my house doing some dishes. My wife had the kids in the living room. We have some thick bushes behind our house. It was so quick that I almost didn't catch it." He took a moment before finishing. "I noticed a branch from one of the trees in the yard." The man stopped at that.

Frank looked at him as though he was kidding. "You got this from a tree branch?" Frank couldn't help himself and began laughing at the man, assuming he was drunker than he realized. Frank stopped himself when he realized no one else was laughing. He brought his head up from the bar top.

The stranger was standing practically on top of Frank. His mood had changed. Every part of his body was aggressive. The sharp eyes looked right at Frank, his lips curled in frustration. "My kid wanted a tree house. The week before, I cleared all those trees to start building one. There were no fucking branches on that tree." The man was seething at Frank.

Frank brought his hands up. "Hey, man, relax. Take a breath. I'm listening."

The stranger sat down, defeated. He ran his right hand through a thick mane of blond hair. The man's chest expanded and recoiled before he began again. "The second time was an hour ago. I usually don't come into the city. I had to drop off paperwork at my accountant's down the street. I saw something but wasn't sure what it was. I came in here to see if he would follow. I offered you a smoke because maybe me pretending to be friends with a cop would scare him off."

Frank sobered up immediately. "Have you seen him since we've been in here?"

The man nodded his head.

"Was he outside?" Frank asked.

The man again nodded his head.

"Is it that homeless guy down the street?"

The man lifted his head. "Did you notice that redhead earlier?"

Frank nodded, remembering he would have liked to know her better.

The man looked around the bar. "That wasn't a woman."

Frank's face lit up, dumbfounded.

The man looked exhausted suddenly. "I gotta go," he said.

With that, the stranger dropped a hundred-dollar bill on the bar and stormed off. Frank immediately wanted to do more for the man.

From the doorway, he heard, "My name's Doug by the way," followed by a door slam.

Frank was ready to leave the encounter as an odd drunken occurrence. He stumbled through the rest of the night thinking of the mysterious "Doug" and the redhead. He fished what was left of the hundred dollars out to buy the rest of his drinks. The man and his story had disappeared from Frank's mind by 7:00 a.m. the next morning. That was nearly twelve years ago.

Doug Collins was found facedown on South Street. When he was turned over, there was nothing left. His eyes, nose, ears, and tongue had been removed. He was handcuffed on both his hands and feet. His scalp down to his chin had been peeled. He'd choked on his own testicles, which were shoved down his throat. Frank learned of this just like the rest of the police department. A gruesome murder like that always became a station story of the week. Frank's guts didn't drop until a picture was posted of what Doug Collins actually looked like. It was the chiseled-chin man from the bar. It wasn't so much that he cared about the victim. He just couldn't risk losing his job right after a divorce had wiped him out financially. Had they found an association between him and the victim, internal affairs would suspend him for an unknown time. Fortunately for him, the case ran cold within a week. Frank breathed a sigh of relief. He had been checking in on the two assigned detectives. They were initially curious about his questions. He explained that his caseload wasn't that bad recently. Frank had known both detectives for many years.

The two South Philadelphia cops were Albert Caggiano and Dominic DeMarinas. Both thought of Frank as the token black man on the force. The Philadelphia Police Department was, in fact, made up of hundreds of African Americans. Frank had been one of the first to reach detective first grade in the early nineties. He'd gotten the gold shield after putting up with fellow cops racist innuendos from day one. He played along after all this time to make sure they stayed off his scent. Both detectives were well past the retirement age—relics of a generation still holding onto the good old days when you could arrest anyone for any reason because there were no cameras. Even the police captain waited with bated breath until the day these guys would retire. The homicide unit was in desperate need of fresh young blood. Frank was confident neither would aggressively chase down a connection.

Because the victim had used cash to pay for his night out, it was particularly difficult to track his route. No bar in the city wanted to be the last place a guy stopped before getting butchered. They started at Monks Café. The bartender never mentioned or just forgot the victim's encounter with Frank. After, they trailed him to Mammoth bar on south street. He was there from 8:30 p.m. until about midnight. The guy had gone there after leaving Frank to drink his bourbons alone.

Frank's hope was that this was the end of it. Neither detective felt the need to look at bars the victim may have visited prior to those times. Frank was hopeful he could put the whole encounter behind him.

Matt Gaetz, nine years ago, was found under the Betsy Ross Bridge. He died from a heart attack brought on by a cattle prod that had been put up his rectum. Ten thousand volts from his ass to his eyeballs until his heart exploded. As heinous as a murder this was, Frank did not see a need to involve himself. Two days after the body was found dangling under the bridge, a man walked into the station. He was a local bartender in the old city neighborhood. He admitted to serving the victim drinks the week prior. He told detectives the man had seemed nervous. He'd claimed someone had been stalking him but had no idea who it might have been. Frank overheard the replay of the bartender's interview while in the coffee room.

Eight months later, Benjamin Sapp was located on the banks of the river. He was reported missing by his wife for two weeks. His throat was cut, and his eyes and lips sewn shut. There were already discussions around this case to leave the file open. Frank was the only detective who knew there was a link. Until a connection was found, it was the police assumption that these people got on the wrong side of whoever. Every time Frank thought maybe he could let it go, someone else showed up.

This time it was a yet unidentified thirty-seven-year-old in the Schuylkill River. The victim was at first identified as a "floater," meaning a drunk of some kind. It wasn't even his case. The other detectives were surprised to see him during the coroner's report. A four-centimeter hole was found on the back of the floater's neck. The coroner explained there was a diamond pattern around it, leading him to believe someone had stuck a Philips head screwdriver directly through his spinal cord. The man had been paralyzed and left to drown. The explanation drew a gasp from all the detectives. Very quickly after, they also collectively decided this case was a wash, because the murder weapon was such a common item. They would work this for a day or two but inevitably walk away from it.

Frank knew deep down he could not just walk away. That man all those years ago had asked him for help, and all he'd done was laugh at him. No point in lying to himself; this would haunt him. Several years before, he had brought the pattern he was beginning to see to the attention of his superiors. What he'd thought might happen was exactly what happened. Every year the police captains were given a budget for their department. That budget depended solely on the number of cases that occurred in their jurisdiction, divided by the number of solved cases. To put it simply, the better police departments got more money. Frank's captain saw this as a financial, not to mention public nightmare. The mere fact that the precinct had not identified or followed a possible serial killer would sink their careers. In short words, Frank was told to let it go.

He wasn't mad, as this was to be expected. He had been around enough to know the deal. His girlfriend at the time was also police. She brought it to Frank's attention that maybe this was a racial disparity. He laughed the suggestion off because, as much as he would like to bring that up, he had to remind her this was Philadelphia. She was a nice girl, and he appreciated the support. However, she was a new cop and didn't fully understand yet that policing was just another business. Everything came down to the dollars. A city budget was really the same as a corporate expense account. The difference was that it was a lot less money and had to cover a lot more people doing a dangerous job. It was tough for a rookie to learn that his or her intentions may be in the right place, but resources were not unlimited.

Frank had been divorced a good long while now. The first year ate at him every day. He was heartbroken but equally furious at the same time. He and his ex-wife had never had kids, a fact now that he was far too grateful for. Kids would have made things even more disastrous. The cataclysmic financial ruin wasn't enough. It coupled with the nightly visions of his ex-wife in bed with his former partner. He knew he was a survivor. He knew from day one of the divorce proceedings that he had to bite down to the bone on it. The pain would eventually pass. It took a long while of sleepless nights and bottomless bottles before it did. If he was being honest with himself, the pain was only unbearable for about six months.

Two years later, he had learned that his former partner had cheated on his former wife. Frank still remembered being drunk with joy that night. The ex had called him in tears, wondering what could have been if only they had worked harder. Frank was too good of a guy not to give her the shoulder to cry on. He drank Macallan 12 on the rocks while she wept on the phone. It was one of the greatest nights of his life.

Nearly ten years later, that phone call still made every day a holiday. The thought of her blubbering tears brought him pure elation whenever he was down. Frank lived in a small ranch house outside of Phoenixville, Pennsylvania. The area used to be a complete shithole, which was why, after the divorce, he'd moved right in. A small rent-to-own house with one bar down the street. It was perfect, he thought. Times had changed dramatically. It was a benefit to him because his now fully owned home had nearly doubled in property value. Young thirtysomethings prized these near-the-city-but-not-in-the-city areas. He knew it didn't really matter because he would never move anyway, but it was still comforting to think about.

This type of independence allowed him to do whatever he wanted in his free time. For a while, it was mostly drinking. Then afternoon drinking became late afternoon cold case curiosity. Now he stared at a vast network of detection in his own house. He still drank here and there but nothing like he had a few years ago. His drive for the regular police work had died off; however, it came back with a vengeance every time he looked at this display. He discovered the drunker he got, the more curious he got. Frank could see things much simpler. The answer to overwhelming was poured over ice.

21

IT'S NOT SO HARD TO SAY GOODBYE

It was no surprise to Lena that her brother and sister were a no-show for Michael Volos's funeral. Over the past ten years, the siblings' relationships had drifted in and out. It occurred to Lena that they had not been together as a family since they were teenagers. Lena had still been married to Mitch the last time she'd seen her parents. He had been a tall, doughy man. He was proud of his knowledge of facts about the world and loved to verbally educate anyone who would listen. Mitch had died at only thirty-six. Lena still thought about him at least once a month.

She remembered the odd way his head was bent and the straggling breaths he took. His legs were flipped over his shoulders. He had fallen so hard but stopped so suddenly. It was terrible for her. She'd waited those last few minutes while he gasped and coughed. The broken spinal column could be seen under the skin of his neck. Blood pooled in the base of his mouth. He'd choked on it, coughing it up into his own face. When he had finally died, she'd let her tears flow naturally down the sides of her face. She had to check his pulse of course before calling the police. As sad as she was to do it, she could not risk him not being dead when they arrived.

After Mitch was Jim. Jim had been a state wrestler with a magnificent body. Jim had shoulders and pectorals carved from marble. He worked out all the time, which she always found to be admirable. Other women would bitch that their husbands were going soft, but not Jim. It had hurt her almost as much as him to drop that barbell into his neck. Jim was in the grips of a major pump. Men never saw it coming. She remembered the look of absolute shock on his face. Only seconds before, he had been bragging to her about the tone of his biceps.

He had brought the bar down to get one last rep in. She'd stood in the corner waiting for him to tire out. When the bar was directly over his head, she'd pounced. He'd pressed as hard as he could with his forearms that looked like twisted rope. Pushing a straight bar loaded with forty-five-pound plates, not to mention a human on top, would have been a world-recorded feat. Jim was strong but not unbreakable.

The tongue was what stood out most. Blue and wet, it kept lashing out like a dog reaching for peanut butter on its nose. His eyes rolled over red. The arteries on his temples nearly popped out of his head. Then it was over. A large blue vein bulged from the center of his forehead—growing so large she thought it might burst into her face. At that moment with Jim flailing under her, his pulsating vasculature reminded her of the Tiber River in Italy. She had looked up pictures and planned to make it a stop during her postmortem trip. She followed the vein from the tip of his forehead until it reached the top of his left eye. Jim's pupils were now pinpoint and unwavering. They looked stuck in place, staring off into the unknown void. He had stopped moving for some time. Her imaginative journey to Italy came to an end; only then did she lift off the bar. She had pushed so hard the bar had indented his neck. She could see his bent trachea wrapping like a hook from underneath.

Lena had formed a routine to avoid suspicion. The first step was ensuring anything she did had complete privacy. Any evidence that could be questioned had to be dealt with quickly. Having now been a part of multiple police investigations, she knew time was the enemy. It was truly amazing what time could tell. When did the heart stop pumping? How hard was it pumping? How old was the blood clotting? When did oxygen leave the body? She had pieced these little facts together while somehow being extremely lucky. Lena was not an idiot. A lot of this came down to circumstance, coupled with a big, beautiful face covered in tears. She was certain some of the detectives had at least suspected her. Time and again, they would just let it go as an accident. To do it right meant you had to create a routine in the house. When the wife had a routine, the husband would follow. From that routine, a person could plan around it. Weeks prior, she had purchased latex gloves and bleach wipes. Her fear was the police finding skin fragments on the opposite side of the bar. They would link those fragments to her. A good forensic examiner would know Jim had not just dropped his weight. Meticulous planning had worked out beautifully for dinner parties, surprise birthdays, and their eventual demise.

Two weeks after Jim imploded on his gym set, Lena met Steve. He was a forty-year-old mama's boy. He was completely useless. Steve liked to be taken care of, which was perfect for Lena. She would create his routine and, therefore, have complete control over his fate. The cutest part about him was that his insecurities made him a misogynistic little bitch. He expected complete subordination. She discovered this about four months into their relationship. She had prepared all day to meet Steve's parents for the first time. Dinner was magnificent. She had dressed the table in white linen cloth. She put out polished metallic candlesticks for ambience. Her playlist for the night was Van Morrison with a little Muddy Waters. There was a nice flow all evening. The meal was superb, roasted duck with Brussels sprouts covered in a light hollandaise sauce.

During the table conversation, Steve's mother had brought up the idea of marriage. Lena smiled, making sure to hold his hand in a dramatic scene of solidarity. "There's no rush. After all, who else would take him?"

Both his parents laughed at the harmless joke.

"We worried about him for a while. Look at him now. He actually might become a man!"

The three of them laughed hardily.

Lena noticed that Steve chuckled as he drank his vodka martini. His father, Clayton Morton the third, expressed his feelings on relationships. "Just keep her in line, son. This one is a wild child. A father can tell."

Steve replied in kind. "She knows her place, Dad."

They smiled at each other, passing this message from father to child. It was a blessed moment of kinship. Two things occurred that only Lena knew. One was that she shuddered with disdain at anyone referencing their child as "son." The second, she felt tremendous heat in her groin from the thought of these parents weeping at young Steve's funeral.

Steve would survive through the holidays. She never liked being alone around the holidays.

For her father's funeral, Lena decided to leave the little boy of a husband at home. She pictured his demise the entire ride to the cemetery. Lena knew this would not be a traumatizing funeral. After arriving, it was slightly jarring to see just how few people were there. Some people she recognized from childhood had shown up. A couple of the odd "friends" stood in the far back from the fresh gravesite.

Most surprising of all was her aunt Mida. Mida and her dad had not spoken in years as far as she knew. She also knew that her mom never talked about Mida. It was as though she'd never existed. Mida, her dad, and her mom never spoke about their past. It was about a year after her family had moved back into Michael and Mida's childhood home. Lena was too young to remember what exactly the fight had been about. According to Christian it was the reason they never saw Mida. Christian could only remember the fight being about a living situation. They assumed their aunt wanted the house instead of their father.

Lena knew her grandparents had died tragically. After that, Mida and her dad had grown in silence. Both of them were in foster care. It was unclear if they lived together. They'd only reconnected when Mida had learned the family had moved back into the house. Mida felt like her home was being stolen from under her. She was appalled that Lena's dad would move his entire family in. Her dad had argued that Mida had not lived in the house for years. She claimed that didn't matter. It was hers as much as his. She didn't care that he had a family to provide for. It was his own fault for taking on the burden of children. The argument was not heard by the children. It was relayed to them over time by their mother.

Lena lost focus on the ceremony. Her aunt drifted over through the already thin crowd. It occurred to Lena that she had not prepared anything for these people. The priest could say his part, and that would be it. While looking away Lena had missed who traveled to her. Mida was now standing directly in front of her. Mida looked at her with what Lena thought at first was a smile. With another second of staring, she saw it obviously wasn't a smile. In fact, she had no idea what the look meant, only that it gave her a feeling of unease.

"Does anyone still live in the house?" Aunt Mida asked.

"No," Lena replied. *What an odd way to start a conversation with the niece you do not know,* she pondered.

"It was never the house's fault. It was your father's," her aunt said.

Lena was taken aback by the remark. "I don't know what you mean."

"Yes, you do. That's why you haven't spoken to your siblings in years—just like I haven't spoken to mine until now when he is gone." Mida glared through Lena, her face still contorting into a look Lena had never seen. "Did you find Mr. Buttersworth?"

"Who?" Lena replied.

The expression on Mida's face made Lena uncomfortable in her bones. Her aunt stared her down before walking away. *Caw! Caw!* The sound came across the small procession. Lena's gaze rested on a telephone pole hanging far above the cemetery plots. In a perfect row sat dozens of dark crows. None of them moved, flapped a wing, or pecked at the air; they only watched her.

Lena stood in place, unsure of what had just happened. A moment came through her mind. She was ten. She had gotten out of bed to get a drink of water. She walked down the hall to the sofa. The night seemed peaceful, so she thought she would read just a little to put herself back to sleep. The couch was an old ratty thing they had acquired years prior. She sat in virtual darkness with just the lamp on that they kept in the corner of the small alcove of the hallway. It was her nature, as it seemed to be in human nature, to always sit on the same part of the sofa. Her spot was on the very end nearest to the stairwell. She liked to listen in on the conversations going on downstairs among her other family members. Rarely was it a conversation involving her siblings. More often than not, it was Mom and Dad deciding on who would be responsible for the kids this week.

Every so often, her mother would bring up Aunt Mida; Dad would quickly shut it down. It was one of the few times he would snap in anger directly at her mother. "*Shhhh,* woman," he would say. Her father never regularly spoke that way. It was only on the subject of Mida that he had no patience.

At this current moment, Lena had the house all to herself. The still quiet of the dark kept her comforted. Cicadas whistled outside in the yard. Every few minutes, the holly tree on the side of the house swiped at the shudders.

She was on chapter two of Pet Cemetery. Church, the family cat, had been run over by a tractor trailer. Louis, the father, was deciding on whether or not to follow Judd, the neighbor, into the Indian burial ground. If it were her cat, she thought, she would leave it for dead and buy a younger one. Her eye caught a movement in the dark. What was that?

The book was laid to rest on her lap as she peered into the room. A dark haze seemed to drift. It was different from the rest of the night. A shadow was in front of her, floating across her vision. She shook her head in confusion, disregarding it. Lena was ready to continue when the movement began. Behind her there was a vibration through the couch. She held the book in her hands, frozen in place. Her stomach turned like an artillery gun, rather than butterfly wings. The vibration was at the floor but slowly continued upward on the back of the couch. She couldn't see well enough when she slowly turned her head.

There it was—the shadow. Fingertips came over the tip of the wooden frame. It could just as easily be a hairless tarantula. She was too terrified to move anyway. It was a black, clouded index finger, followed by the rest that began to crawl over her shoulder. The fingers became a hand that gripped her hair and then slowly clawed her shoulder. The hand closed on her shoulder with nails cutting into her skin. She could feel the blood coming from the lacerations. Lena didn't move, didn't scream; she refused to acknowledge the fear that held her.

Then the bite came. Something had her by the back of her neck. It cut deep with what felt like razor blades for teeth. It bit her once and then sniffed at her hair. "Want some candy?" the voice asked in her ear.

Another bite, this one into the back of her head. The skin under her hair pulled back with tension. Lena spurted out cries. Saltwater welled up under her eyelids. The shadow slowly sank away behind her. In the dark she heard it again. "The smell," it said.

Lena had sat in a paralyzed state until the sun came up. The book had remained in her lap open to the same page for hours. She had never learned what had happened to the cat.

22

FUCK BANSHEES

Christian sometimes asked himself if he could come back like an invisible spirit to observe the lunacy of the living. He wanted to have a legacy to himself—not one for other people to remember. He wanted to be a watcher from the walls, ever aware even after he was long dead. He had no desire to involve himself in the lives of others. He had his lists of things to do and people to see. He wanted to remain left alone and to die alone, having never been acknowledged by another living soul. As he thought about this, he realized how hypocritical he was in his own actions. He had been involving himself more into people's lives than the average person in a full lifetime.

Right now, in fact, he stood in the dark behind a pine tree. The figures in the house moved from room to room—a man, a woman, two children; it was beautiful, he thought. They were all so blissfully unaware, of anything. He knew the woman. She was Ashley Graham of the Graham household with the Graham kids and the Graham husband. Twenty-five years ago, she had been Ashley Wilson. Ashley had been known for her boisterous personality. She was able to command children and incite crowds. She never did anything to Christian. Ashley was so powerful that she brought an entire class of twelve-year-old kids down on a boy named Jeremy. Jeremy had a stutter. Jeremy could not even put together a sentence to protect himself against a force like Ashley. Christian had always been mad at himself for standing idly by while Ashley tormented the helpless kid.

Jeremy had not shown up to school one day. He had decided to do something about the bullying. A day after Ashley's taunts, Jeremy had walked all the way home and up to his room; broken his bedroom window; and thrown himself, headfirst, out of it.

Christian now watched the same bubbly girl act as a bubbly mom and wife. In the comic strip he had created for Ashley, she'd played the Blond Banshee. In the story, she'd screamed so loudly that young, frightened dwarves would explode upon hearing her shriek. The dwarves lived in the land of fortitude. In this land, all life was held in a high regard. The land was plentiful with grasses and vegetation. Deer and moose roamed freely, eating at the berries that fell off dogwood trees. The sun rose every day and cast a magnificent pinkish sunset every night. The dwarves gathered on hilltops with their dwarf families to see the end of the day.

The night was a different story all together. If just one of them left their dwelling, they put themselves at risk of the banshee. The Blond Banshee hovered above, waiting for the weak ones who did not make it home before the sun went down. Many nights, she attacked the old ones too confused to stay in their hut. Within their homes, the dwarves could feel the wind from her flying drift into their windows. Sometimes out of sheer boredom, the banshee would grab a child nearest the window and fly high into the night sky with it. She would continue up until the air became like ice. From the dark space, she would drop the child. Once while having her fun, she accidentally dropped one right onto its own father's head. He was looking up desperately awaiting the arrival of his baby. Together they lay, in a crushed mass outside their own home.

The villagers finally took control of their homeland with a dirty little trick. An elder dwarf had decided his time on the earth was at its end. He volunteered to be of service for the survival of the community. He waited until dark one evening after a particularly beautiful sunset. The villagers watched from their closed windows. The man feigned confused and weak, of which he was neither.

The banshee came from the distant sky, a dark smile across her pale face. She shrieked and heckled the man. He turned in circles as though unsure of his surroundings. The banshee grabbed him by the back of his neck with her long black fingernails. She ascended the clouds, mocking him the whole way. The old dwarf said nothing. She flew higher and higher, waiting for his pleas for mercy. Finally, she held him tight but circled to look at him face-to-face.

Together, they hovered in the icy night sky. "Why are you not begging, little dwarf?" she bellowed. "Aren't you afraid!?"

The old man lifted his head, staring his people's enemy in the eye. "Because today we are larger than you." And with that, the dwarf pulled a long silver hook from his coat. He swung it once at the banshee's cheek. The hook sliced through her face as she screamed in painful surprise.

She dropped the old man, who held on to the chain attached to the hook, and together they descended back to earth—the banshee screaming, waving her hands at nothing. The old man held on with his eyes closed. Contentment hugged him like a warm cloth. The banshee plummeted to her death as a result of her own cruelty.

Christian breathed in the cool night air, replaying the story of the old dwarf in his head. It occurred to him for the first time that in this story the villain lost. He wondered if maybe he wanted all villains to lose? Maybe he was too young in the early stories to know how to beat them? He was not too young anymore. *Today I kill a banshee*, he thought.

Fortunately, Ashley had held on to her teenage habit of smoking. The first few weeks of reconnaissance, he'd noticed she snuck off whenever possible. Her husband knew, but Christian wondered if the kids were aware Mommy was a smoker. Christian waited in this quiet, dark place behind the tree. This was his favorite place in the whole world—the black balaclava covering his head and face, the feel of his serrated knife in his back pocket, the instrument of destruction in his right hand. Christian had read for years about the science of sociopaths, psychopaths, bipolarity, and every other disorder to explain why people did bad things. His realization was that he may or may not have a number of those conditions. It did not matter, not to him. The things he did were justified according to the laws of humanity. He never felt remorse or regret. The acts were justified. His victims were the rude cunts of humanity. His sole purpose was to eradicate them. Here he waited patiently in the dark. Christian always took a moment before making his move to meditate on the choice. It always came back the same, as nothing. Nothing in his entire body was trying to stop him from this act of violence.

Ashley was taking the last drag off her Parliament Light. Her favorite part of the day was coming out for a smoke, away from the rest of the world. Life had become so boring that this small relief was all she looked forward to. She'd known who

Bill was when she'd married him—tall, dull, insecure. She was fully aware her kids were little versions of herself. They would conquer the world but always knew who ran the show. She had every reason to be satisfied with the suburban soccer mom monotony. Plus, the little affairs on the side always kept things interesting. Bill was such a blind pussy he never knew a thing. He should be too grateful for having a woman as beautiful as her in his life.

Ashley enjoyed the control she had over her world. Suburbia was boring and easy to manipulate. Here, there was no room for people she considered less than. Every so often, a new young couple would move in with their ideas of social equality, liberalism, unjust systemic racism, and other bullshit. The neighbors had Ashley to thank for running out the intruders within months, maybe a year. As the head of the PTA she would make sure the new people's children were singled out in every class. Since Bill was a member of the city council, it was all too easy making sure construction projects always popped up within earshot of their house. The young idealists never knew why life became so hard so fast. Ashley smiled with satisfaction at the thought.

She was too busy dwelling on how perfect everything was to notice the shadow move to her side. Christian came around the corner, hand already out with a titanium baton. She never saw the metal stick as it crashed into the left side of her eye. The world went dark. Ashley felt blood fill her head. She was being dragged along the ground. She heard small grunts but couldn't open her eyes. Her forehead pounded like it was going to explode. *What the fuck just happened?* she thought. *Wake up,* she yelled at herself. *Wake up.*

Her eyes fluttered open. The pounding in her temple was unbearable. It took her several seconds to focus her sight. There above her was a man in the dark. Anger flashed through every nerve in her body. She tried to yell. Her mouth wasn't working correctly yet. The man's head drooped a little to the left. *What is he doing?* she thought. "Do you fuckin' know me. I'll kill you, motherfucker!" she screamed. Words came out jumbled. The feeling in her jaw had come back to her. The bone crunched against gums. Pain burst through her mouth. "Where am, I asshole?" Tears flew from her eyes, mixing with bloody spit from her swollen mouth.

Christian had dug the hole a week before near the Philadelphia Airport. The hole was lined with wood he had collected out of the back of a Home Depot. He watched Ashley taking in her current surrounding. Her reaction was exactly what he assumed it would be. She poured insults at him. Not once did she acknowledge her complete vulnerability in the situation. Godzilla had come to life to eat this little creature. That was what she could not comprehend. For the first time in Ashley's life, she was the prey. When her eyes finally locked on Christian's, he said only three words. "Jeremy is watching."

Christian slammed the large wooden lid on the hole and quickly used a nail gun to seal it. She punched at the wood plank with all her strength; her wrist cracked. She punched again and again, breaking one maybe both wrists along with some fingers. The pain radiated up both arms. She had just taken away her only weapons. Ashley watched in the dark, still taking in the horror around her. The moonlight casted a shadow around the man. She followed the beams of light from corner to corner. The light shining through small cracks in the coffin gave her hope. The dirt seeping through from his shovel took that hope away. He was burying her in here. The shock grabbed her like a vice around her throat. Another scream had reached her vocal cords and was nearing her lips when she felt the ground moving.

The movement was stealthy. It started by her head but traveled down toward her feet. The ground came alive. Christian had begun throwing dirt over the hole. With each shovelful, he awaited what would be the inevitable screaming. First, there was shuffling. The shuffling joined a whimper. He imagined in his mind how hard Ashley must be straining to see right now. Then screams came. No words, only guttural cries. He had dropped a collection of multilegged horrors to keep her company. None of it would be fast, as she deserved a lengthy death. He had slowly stolen the creatures from the anthropology department of the zoo. A Brazilian centipede supposedly with the most painful bite of all insects, a wolf spider from Australia, and a bark scorpion from South America.

Ashley bellowed. With each cry, Christian considered which creature she was experiencing. There was no doubt when the centipede got ahold of her. Christian had never heard pleading so loud in all his life. In his research, he had learned the centipedes bite was so painful it could lead to cardiac arrest. He piled the dirt higher; the wailing never stopped. He took a moment before doling out the last shovelful of dirt to hear her cries coming from below.

Christian felt eyes on him. From his left corner in the trees sat hundreds of yellow eyes. None of them moved after being noticed. The stillness only eased with the sound of Ashley's murmurs. Crows of all sizes, black as the air around them watched. *Caw! Caw!* came only once from the audience.

23

SANTA SUCKS

Natalie always thought the day would come that she would make the journey home. The truth was distance had been a warm blanket. She valued a life of complete independence. She had watched the medical students and physician attendings pass through her life, thinking they could make her "the one." At times, she felt bad to disappoint them. That inevitably disappeared. Natalie could never understand why they would want to pursue a relationship with her. Their emotions always got the better of them. She did not find it pathetic. It was just so odd. She had made it through her undergrad with minimal attention. There had been occasional flings, all kept in secret. Medical school was more complicated because she was part of a team of residents who spent endless hours, even years together. Her true satisfaction came when residency finally ended. So many of these people had originally gone into medicine with good intentions. They came from all backgrounds throughout the world. The goal was to help people in any way they could.

Everyone knew that being a doctor no longer came with the prestige it once had twenty or thirty years ago. Doctors were now expected to sign on with major health networks that incorporated multiple community and university hospitals. During their residencies, they interviewed with physician groups that worked with these hospital networks. In simple terms, they were labor unions for physicians.

Toward the end of their tenure, many of her fellow medical students had lost that initial spark. They realized their careers would, in fact, be more about avoiding lawsuits. It was not all so negative. The majority still enjoyed their specialties and looked forward to advancing their skills. The difficult part was realizing no real acknowledgment would come their way.

Natalie had her own intentions. This was never an issue for her. She had noticed from the very beginning while taking care of patients how many were kept alive for others. Their families were too weak to make the hard decisions. Sometimes, the families who claimed to love their dying relatives so much were sucking up social security benefits. The patients did not want to be here. It was not their choice. The patients had tubes in places no one would ever want tubes. They had become medical experiments, poked and bled all day every day. Hammered with radiation to see if their chronic problem had subsided, only to have their hearts broken. She had concluded, most hated to find out they were still sick, not because they were sick but because the torture to heal them would continue. It was in year two of her residency that she began making decisions for her patients.

Her first victim was a ninety-year-old man. He had a breathing tube, a rectal tube, a nasogastric tube, and more IV lines than most people could count. The nurses had to wipe away his tears every time they moved him. Movement reopened one of his thousand bedsores. It was his piece of shit family that had done this to him. They claimed, "This is what he would want." No one alive would ever want this type of treatment. Day in and out, the family argued with medical workers to continue the torture.

It was on a night shift that Natalie had decided to make a move. The man was breathing through a ventilator. Ventilators used pressure and volume to adequately breathe for a human being. Fortunately, there were no cameras located in the room. If something did happen, it would never be investigated, due to his age and disease process. At 3:00 a.m., while everyone on the staff was struggling to stay awake, Natalie quickly bolted into the room. She turned the volume in liters of air from 500 to 1,000. She had watched the respiratory therapists work the dials every day. The comparison was blowing into a balloon right as it was about to pop. She knew a quick turn followed by a confirm button was all she needed to do.

What happened next went very quickly. Fragile patients lose lung compliance. "Compliance" was the term to describe how pliable lungs were. The older a person gets, the less flexible the lungs become. "Barotrauma" was a term used to describe injuries that resulted from care in a patient's thoracic region. One of the greatest fears in hospital ICUs is placing too much air into a patient's chest. A pneumothorax is a type of barotrauma from too much pressure on dry lungs. These are the things Natalie kept in mind. Upon inhalation of the air, both lungs blew open, causing a tension pneumothorax. The lobes that made up a person's lungs would pop like balloons at a birthday party.

Alarms sounded across the board, and staff members awoke from the night shift trance and raced into the room. Natalie had hidden herself behind the curtain of the adjoining room. She waited until the last nurse had run past to come out at a quick pace. She followed in the back of the crowd, keeping her presence to a minimum. Fortunately, there were other residents and attending doctors already working on the man. She was not needed.

Internally, his blown lungs pulled on his aorta, causing myocardial infarction also known as a heart attack. In that short amount of time, Natalie had saved the man from another day of hell. Pride in her work provided calm to her mind.

Natalie had taken care of multiple patients in need over the last couple of years. She felt maybe now was a good time to get some distance. Her father's death was a good excuse to get away—not that she had any desire to go home. The memories for her remained in a cloudy haze. She only remembered the anxiety all day waiting for what might happen at night. She remembered counting down the hours until the day she moved out. She was young and felt weak in her parents presence. Not only did her parents not respond to their children's pleas for help; they seemed to revel their fear.

Natalie touched her neck on the left side just under her carotid artery. Christmas Eve 1990, she had waited by the steps to see if Santa was real or just a story for younger kids. It seemed nothing in the world was more important to her at that moment. She waited in the dark, crouched under the corner table. She had turned off the light so Santa wouldn't see her. Like any kid, Natalie imagined hearing the sound of reindeer steps landing on the roof. The fireplace would start to shake a little as Santa clambered down the brick interior. He might even get stuck with the big bag of presents he was bringing. The future doctor in her was very curious how such a rotund man planned to get down a skinny chimney. She had been so good all year no matter what. They had all been good. Natalie hoped one of his gifts was a pair of rollerblades. The image of skating through the neighborhood danced across her mind.

"The little girl is sitting alone, Mother."

The darkness rests behind the tree. The little girl is seen at the top of the steps.

"She is waiting for their gift giver, my child."

A shadow moves behind the girl. A figure is near her in the dark.

"Our friend has come to play with the girl, Mother."

"Yes, my child. Let us watch."

Natalie remembered opening her eyes and realizing she had fallen asleep. Presents were under the tree. *Oh no*, she thought. She was so mad at herself. There was a good amount of presents but not the haul she was hoping for. A clicking sound was happening somewhere. Maybe Santa was still in the house!

From the dark hallway came the voice. "Smells," was all it said in a hiss.

She froze in place, still crouched with her arms pulled in tight to her chest. "Santa," Natalie said. "Santa, where are you?"

She felt a brushing along her neck. There was something around her throat. It felt like wire, it was moving, tightening around her. It began to squeeze; now panic was setting in. She reached up, but the wire was already cutting into her skin. She couldn't take a breath or let one out. Her face began to swell; she felt her eyes go wide. She flailed, reaching into the dark to find who was holding it but felt nothing—just a wire on its own strangling her. The world went dark as her eyes closed.

She heard it again, but it seemed farther away. "I smelled you," was what it said.

Natalie had awoken gasping for air. Lena had been standing over her with a towel on her neck. Natalie was breathing so fast it took all her will to slow herself down. She let out multiple dry coughs and held Lena's hand with the towel. The pain in her chest and throat overtook her thoughts of Christmas. The girls looked at each other. Natalie never thought about Santa clause again.

24

TRUE DETECTIVE

It happened during many complicated homicide cases. Frank had to take a step back for a new look at everything. He decided this was the time for that. The moving parts became blurred. Put the facts out in front. Look at everything fresh. So far, he had nine victims over the last eleven years. Unbeknownst to his colleagues, Frank had taken up part of his own garage and made it into his private research area. Over the years, he had taken copies of evidence associated with the nine murders. Frank had two folded-out tables littered with scraps of evidence. Some of it was local newspaper clippings. Other items were official documents he'd gotten ahold of in exchange for the promise of a favor to other cops. It's not that the police force was ignoring the possibility that there was an active serial killer. The truth was that manpower was low. Half of the possibly related cases were in different jurisdictions over long periods of time. Here in his private sanctuary, Frank could lay out case after case, hoping to connect the dots. The cases included those of Kevin

McCarthy, Doug Collins, Matt Gaetz, and Kelly Conway. Mrs. Conway was murdered in 2005. She had been bound at the feet and hands, thrown into a dumpster, and set ablaze. The second was that same year but six months later. Kevin McCarthy had washed up on LBI in Jersey. Mr. McCarthy had a bad Fourth of July. He went missing from a beach party and was found the next day with his cock and balls removed, made to bleed out.

All were the same age. All were from the Philly area born and raised. Most were college educated; however, the colleges had no decisive pattern. One was Boston College, the other Villanova, and so on. They were married with kids. Kevin lived in Haddonfield, New Jersey, and Kelly in Westchester, PA. The age was what kept nagging at him. Clearly there was a connection in time. Rather than try to pull details from all the suspected cases, Frank decided to pick the ones found close together. If a pattern emerged from a couple, there was a good chance the rest would follow. What about their parents? In the original interviews, it had been determined that Kevin's parents lived in northeast Philly and Kelly's in Old City. However, he noticed a note written under the second page that read, "Parents moved in '97." So where had they lived before?

Frank reached out to Kelly's mother. Her mother was not pleased to be hearing from another detective—especially one with no answers. Frank could never imagine the pain these families must go through waiting for answers.

Prior to 1997, Kelly's family had been living in the northeast region of Philly. The two had not attended high school together, because Kevin was at private school and Kelly at public. Both had attended St. Catherine Middle School in the early '90s. Frank asked Kelly's mother if she had been part of any extracurricular activities. Her mother impressed upon him that she had been part of every club and sport. She was an outgoing girl with a knack for making friends. The mother kept shoving this idea at Frank. He began to wonder if she was the kind who made enemies as easily as friends. If she was as pushy as her mother, that might be the case. This could be the connection. Did that apply to the other victims?

The bodies had been discovered in Philadelphia, Jersey, and Delaware. Clearly the suspect had a tie to the area. Going over the investigation files, Frank realized most background checks were incomplete. To be fair to his fellow investigators, high school was usually as far back as they would go. The victims were the same age range, meaning they would have been in the classes at the same time. Who had they sat next to? Did these murders go back to one incident or a string of incidents? Was this the result of bullying? He had to sit back and think about the depth of this background. These were heinous crimes. Could it all really have come from schoolyard battles?

Victims three, four, and five all check out as having lived within the northeast region of the city. Doug Collins, the victim who'd started all this for Frank, had also lived in that section of the city as a child. Frank remembered one of the detectives mentioning the Catholic youth league's basketball team. St. Catherine's was part of the CYO team league. It was not a stretch to assume Doug Collins had also gone to St. Catherine's.

Frank spent the next few hours going over old interviews from family members. He was about ready to crack a Yuengling open when it hit him that nothing in all the files was from a teacher. The lazy pair assigned to the cases had never driven out there. He closed the fridge, grabbed his car keys, and headed out the door. On the GPS, he could see that St. Catherine's was in the Kensington section of the city, about a twenty-minute drive.

It was already three thirty that afternoon. If his memory from middle school was correct, it meant school would be empty soon. Frank made a rush of it, blowing through most lights all the way up Broad Street. He cut left on Girard Avenue and followed the old trolley tracks into Kensington. He hadn't been in this section in a long time. He was reminded of what the city must have looked like after the boys came home from World War II—miles of old lots that today were completely unaffordable and now renovated to be multifamily homes The old wood architecture with a huge sprinkle of Pennsylvania Dutch was part of them all. If it wasn't for the tire shops and liquor stores you could almost imagine being in Amish country.

He kept driving until the lawns got a smidge nicer but not too nice. The homes were now suburban ranches with a less city feel. He drove several blocks and made a left on Norris street. There stood an old brick church. He read the sign out front. "St. Catherine of Sienna, Repent, for the Day is Dark."

Why the fuck did Catholicism have to be so goddamn ominous? he thought. Was life not hard enough that people needed to be reminded they were probably screwing up the fictional afterlife? That was a conversation for another day, he told himself.

Frank found a parking spot next to the priest rectory section. He did not get out of the car. His adrenaline had taken over his logical reasoning. If he walked in to open a line of questioning, this could easily ruin a case—through word of mouth maybe even scare a suspect into hiding. He had this, and no one else did. The school was not going anywhere. He needed more evidence before involving others.

25

FRIEND OF THE DEVIL

Lena decided to head back to their Derry Street home. Her stomach began to turn when she was still over a mile away. What had her aunt meant? "It wasn't the house." What kind of statement was that? She found herself angrier than she realized—she had not seen that woman in thirty years and that was her only remark. "Bitch," she said out loud in the car.

She made the final turn down the suburb drive. Small flashes of childhood ran through her mind—a bike ride down that alley behind the old couple's house, stalking the neighbors at night, sneaking out of the house as a teenager, and so on. Even one or two encounters with the cops. It usually involved Christian and his stupidity. Lena drove the last quarter mile until she sat right in front of home sweet home. Childhood homes always look smaller when you see them as adults, and this moment was no different. Lena felt the hair on her neck shoot up.

An old habit made her go in through the back screened porch. The door creaked desperately for some WD-40. Most of the screens were torn or rusted through. The lawn was completely overrun. Ivy and moss had crawled up the siding all the way to the roof. There was not a doubt in her mind that the neighbors definitely considered this place an eyesore. The back screen door was off the hinges and hanging on by what looked like a coat hanger. She walked through into the kitchen entrance.

The place had become a squat house. The wallpaper was peeled and stained throughout. The countertops were littered with broken things, dead bugs, and random burn marks. The smell was a mix of mildew and spilled beer. She walked through the house, not recognizing any of it. The rooms were the same, but it was now a litter box. She felt a slight twinge of guilt for not getting her dad out sooner. This was a place where her family had lived. It had not been the safest living situation, knowing what hunted them at night. It was still home. Now it had gone to rot.

The kids knew there was something in the house watching them. It was always fearful to be alone or to find yourself in the dark. For them, monsters were real. Lena knew what was in these rooms, both downstairs and up. She turned from the living room and decided to head to the basement. Through the dark, she could see the dangling light bulb. She reached for it and was greeted by the walls of concrete and dust. Her childhood came flooding back. How many times had they found Christian down here cowering in a corner? He would always be wearing a new mark of some kind, a bite, strange cuts, always paralyzed with fear. He would never say what had happened. They never needed him to.

She headed toward the back workshop. Under the bench covered in dirt there were steno notebooks sticking out. Christian had made his stories down here. She grabbed the top book and rifled through. The front page was labeled "5 Grade." There was a list of about twenty kids, written at different times with different ink or pencil. She remembered how he'd always carried one of these with him. Next to each name was a brief account of something the kid had done. It looked like he had also left markers to symbolize something. Some had red stars next to their name; others had black stars. She scanned down. One name was written in black with a red star drawn around it. It read, "Matt Gaetz: Matt stole Jamie's lunch money every day. Jamie cried when Matt punched him. Jamie tried to yell, but he talks funny. Matt, Jim, Ashley laughed at him."

For a moment, she thought maybe it had all been in her head. Maybe their imaginations had gotten the better of the three of them. She moved to go back upstairs, she pulled on the light cord, and history became reality. The three of them had been playing hide-and-seek before the Fourth of July. It was hot out, and all the doors and windows of the house had been left open. They'd started in the backyard, scattering to find good hiding spots.

Lena was sure that Christian had gone into the basement, and so she came trouncing down the stairs after him. Sure enough, she found him hiding behind the dryer against the back wall. Natalie yelled from the kitchen, "Are you guys down there?"

"Yeah!" they yelled. "Come on down."

There was silence. They both waited to hear Natalie's footsteps, but there was no sound.

They heard a gasp and then a crash. A cooking pot came bouncing down the stairs and took them by surprise. They both jumped back with shock. Christian went to pick up the pot, he was knocked down by a larger object hurled down the steps. Lena looked, and it was Natalie. Christian lay flat on his stomach. Lena had to help him turn the unconscious girl. She was bleeding from her head. The door to the upstairs slammed shut. Christian and Lena looked up, eyes wide.

Christian said, "The doors were open. It was probably just wind."

Then they heard the scratching on the other side. Something was leaning on the door from the kitchen. They were silent.

"I smell you," a voice said from the other side.

They stood paralyzed for what seemed like days but was truly only seconds. Finally, Lena reached out her hand to pull the light cord. She cut the tip of her index finger, realizing poor Natalie had been thrown right into the light. She stepped forward and felt lightbulb glass crack under her shoes.

They'd stayed there in the dark for the rest of the night. No more hide-and-go-seek games.

Lena stood at the bottom of the steps all these years later. The memory washed through every part of her. She took a long breath and opened her eyes for a final glance at this dark place. Something caught her attention. The light from the bulb stopped at the walls around the entire basement except for one spot. She walked over to the corner where the washer and dryer used to sit. There, along the wall in the corner, was a large gap in the concrete. She peered closer and walked forward toward it. The corner was missing a three-foot section of wall. Brick had been pulled out at the very bottom by the floor. How long had this been there? she wondered.

Lena brought her phone out, for the small light bulb only helped so much in the dark down here. She turned on her flashlight and put it right onto the gap. She had to squat down to look through. The cutout of rock was smooth from water damage, meaning it had been here for decades. The hole went back another three feet. There in the dark was the strangest thing, a pillow and blanket. There was something else too. Was that a dead animal? No, Lena could make it out even under all the dirt. It was a stuffed rabbit doll. *How in the hell did these things wind up in the wall?* she thought. But she took the time to really look at the items. Both had a two-inch layer of dirt on them. It was obvious they had been here a long time. Lena backed away from the hole, surveying the wall. How had they missed this? Clearly this had been here for years.

Then it hit her. The washer and dryer sat in front of this part of the wall. Just to the left of the gap sat the water attachment. With both of those here, there would be no way to see this, especially in the dark. She headed back to the stairs, letting this slowly sink in. She stopped in her tracks. Lena looked again at the hole, not really being able to see it in the dark. Out loud she asked the question, "Are you Mr. Buttersworth?"

"The woman found the toy, Mother."

"Yes, my child. She is a woman now. She was a little girl in this place once."

Lena was into the wall up to her waist. Behind her in the stillness a cloud lingered by the dusty light bulb.

"She is dangerous now, my child. The creature stalked her at night. It helped us shape her. Now she kills without remorse."

The cloud watched Lena pull herself out of the hole. She made her way back up the stairs and was gone.

"She has become a devil to men, my child."

"I hope we see the others, Mother."

"It is no matter, my child. The spirits have turned a blind eye to their wickedness. We are avenged tenfold."

26

TRUCKIN'

Christian decided to take a little time off. He struggled to think of all the people he still had on his list who needed to be taken care of. So many rude, wicked people with no sense of how to treat another human. Some, like Ashley, were the worst. They appealed to others similar to themselves. They portrayed socioeconomic perfection, while hidden away was pure evil. They surround themselves with glamorous people blatantly spouting racist, narrow-minded views they took as intelligence. If the opportunity would only present itself, he would bury them all. Christian had tried not to create a scene too often in the city. It had been over a decade, and still, no one had ever knocked on his door or followed him down the street looking for a body. He was sometimes astounded that there was no mention of his acts being connected. Yes, they were done in different states. Yes, they were all different actions. But still it shocked him the pieces had not come together. He had no desire to stop but had learned that time away was good for his health, not to mention his freedom.

Knowing his father was dead brought a great calm over his body. This was probably as good a time as any for a trip into the past. He packed just a few things in a bag, along with his toolkit, and hit the road. It had now taken him thirteen years to go back. He figured he would do some camping for a few days and just cut himself off for a while. The Pocono Mountains were not far away. Blue Mountain served as a trailhead to the great Appalachian Trail. If he was truly inspired, maybe a three-month hike down to Georgia would be fun. He knew himself too well. The hike would be enjoyable for a few days, but eventually, he would feel unproductive. He drove up the turnpike, for most of the way in complete silence. The hum of the wind with the windows down was always a good reprieve from the drone of human interaction. Too much noise had clouded his mind. He had not realized how tightly wound he was until right now, when he could focus on nothing, just the road ahead.

He pulled up to the house. He had expected to feel an emotional roller coaster in the core of his gut. Oddly enough, he felt nothing. Memories passed through his mind—nothing that brought him nostalgia, depression, nothing at all. In fact, he had come to realize the only times he felt true emotion was when he was inflicting justified retribution on anyone on his list. When was the last time he had felt a real emotion without outside stimulus? Would he ever feel an emotion again? More importantly, did he even want to?

Christian pulled up to the front yard, noticing a new BMW in the driveway. It had to be Lena. She was always particular. The house was clearly in decay. It gave him the urge to walk back and drive away. Oddly enough, he felt something pulling him in. The front door creaked open. A woman came walking out carrying her head high—regardless of the fact she'd just exited what looked like a crack den. Without a doubt, there she was. This was his sister. Lena was also the woman who several men had paid the ultimate sacrifice for. He smiled on the inside with pride at her work. She had always been so calculating. He felt that, in order to accomplish what he wanted, it meant cutting off the world. Lena had learned to do it as a member of society—and not just any member either, but a successful one.

They approached each other in the overgrown grass of the front yard. Lena eyed Christian up and down; he looked mildly disheveled but altogether healthy. Christian noticed the massive ring that swung with her hand. *Poor bastard*, he thought. He smiled again on the inside. They stared awkwardly at each other, not at a loss for words, just comfortable in the same space.

Lena motioned with a head tilt, "Looks like shit in there,"

"Not much better out here," Christian replied.

Together they eyed the overgrown front yard.

"What are you doing here?" she asked.

He never considered why he'd come home. "I just wanted to know how it would feel to come back." Christian looked toward the roof of the house. He blinked a few times in the mild sunlight. They stood in silence for a little while longer. "Why didn't they move? Why did they keep us in this place? They knew we were scared, but they never did anything for us." Christian pondered these questions, never taking his gaze off the roof.

Lena knew that statement was the entire essence of Christian's being. She knew without saying it that the hauntings had never left him. "We were kids, brother. We were scared of the dark, and sometimes, we probably just tried to scare each other." Lena had been able to justify their nightmares this way after several counseling sessions in her early twenties. "Our minds have probably exaggerated those memories anyway. They were all nightmare stories that we have unknowingly and subconsciously embellished."

Christian looked straight through her. His features became much darker. Suddenly she felt unsafe in front of him. "You know that isn't true. You know, as Natalie and I know, that this place has bad earth. You know that we were tormented by something in this house. Feed that to your soon-to-be-dead husband; don't ever bring that to me."

Lena felt weak and stupid. He was right. She was trying to explain away facts. "It's been so long since we talked. I forgot we were a team. The last decade has made me feel very alone."

Christian's glare at her softened. His shoulders relaxed. He took a breath. "I know, but you're not alone."

Lena took steps toward him. "It good to see you." She took hold of his arm. "I hope to see you again." She walked past him toward the driveway.

Christian stood looking at the front door. He couldn't decide if going back in really served a purpose. Behind him, Lena's car pulled out and drove off. Christian whispered to himself, "It was good to see you too. I am sorry to never see you again."

The house could see them now in the sunlight clear as day. It recognized them instantly. Brother and sister back again to see their home. The shudders creaked with delight. The gutter released water droplets down the sides, trying to clean off the muck resting on its siding. The windowpanes tried to clear themselves of dust to allow in more light. *Come see how good it looks inside*, the house thought. *Leave the door open just a little while longer so the wind can carry away the leaves on the floor. Open all the windows so that the sun may dry up the mold now crowding in the corners of all the rooms. Just stay awhile,* it thought. *Come see how happy the home can be.*

Christian stood a little while longer surveying the property. He paced around to the back, allowing smells from the holly tree to enter his mind. Then he felt it. He was being watched. In his core, he knew it. Stillness surrounded him in the backyard. The breeze died off. *Thump, thump, thump,* went his heart. The sun cast pink and orange across the yard. There in the window above the holly tree was darkness. Nothing was there. No lights were on; of course, there was darkness in the window. Christian stared, forcing his eyes to not blink. The dark was staring back.

"We missed him, Mother."

"Yes, my child. The man who was a boy. He is now a demon."

The dark cloud wavered slightly in a narrow corner.

"We see you, boy. You are so dangerous. We are so proud of you."

Christian stood still in the grass. *You have always been there watching me,* he thought.

Lena drove down the highway heading back to her suburban life. Christian was right, she felt bad for having tried to make light of it in front of him. It hadn't been childish make-believe; something did go bump in the night. The house had cursed them. She knew what Christian had been up to all these years. They never spoke, but every so often, an article or newsfeed would pop up, and she just knew it was him. It was the same with Natalie. Every six months or so, there would be a small story about a young tragedy at the hospital. She figured there were probably many more that she had no clue about. Not that she was a saint. None of them were saints.

It was her parents' fault for not taking them away. It was God's fault for letting that house be built on soiled ground. She couldn't help but think about her aunt's words. "It wasn't the house." What the fuck did that mean? They had lived there, had seen what they'd seen, and they'd survived it, only to be fucked-up human adults. Also, where the hell had her aunt been all those years? *Fuck you, bitch*, Lena thought.

Lena turned the car around. She wanted answers.

27

5 STARS

Natalie lay in the hotel bed, fully clothed. She had checked in, come immediately to her room, and lain down. Here she stayed, just staring at the ceiling in complete silence. It was strange to think how not often a person was surrounded by complete silence. She closed her eyes to embrace the bliss. She was following the lines of blood under her eyelids, allowing the white and red pattern movements to rock her into a lull. The little resident named Tao Sung popped into her mind. He'd followed her around day and night while on her residency in Montana. The poor guy had picked Montana of all places for his first visit to the United States. Not only that, he had picked the smaller of the university hospitals outside of Beaumont to do his residency. He'd stood out loudly among the white mountain people. It was unfortunate too because he was clearly intelligent and would have been a capable doctor.

She took pity on him one night while they both covered the emergency department. Nothing exciting had come through the door for the last nine hours. It was now 3:00 a.m., so Natalie had decided on a fourth cup of coffee. She wandered into the physician break room to find Tao crying into his folded arms. Natalie was never good with emotion. It suited her emergency care career very well. Emotion was the roadblock to decision making. In a rare moment of empathy, she walked over and sat next to him.

Tao looked up at her, eyes red, filled with tears. His English was good—not good enough to be counted among the local population. "Are all Americans this mean?" he asked through teary lips.

Without giving it a second thought, she reached into his scrub bottoms. Natalie grabbed hold of everything he had. Tao jumped back terrified. Natalie only stared at him, not speaking. Tao remained motionless, fearful of the entire situation. She began to pull at him gently. His look grew calmer; he kept his hands on the edge of the table still not sure how to react. Natalie kept rubbing and pulling. Tao's faced contorted between fear and pleasure. Only a minute later did he explode into his pants. He crashed forward onto the table, trying to hold in a loud groan. His head now rested on his arms, still soaked in tears.

He panted and, under his breath, asked, "Why?"

Natalie leaned into his ear. "A going away present. They will never accept you here."

The crash next door woke her from the daydream. Annoyed and a little confused, Natalie leaned her head closer to the wall above the bed. There was thunderous yelling from the other side. It was a man clearly on a heated phone call. She could guess who it was with. In a distant roar, she could hear, "I put fuckin' food on the table. I provide, you ungrateful bitch!"

Natalie continued to lay still, listening more and more intently. She giggled, feeling like a secret part of the argument.

The man went on and on, his voice getting perpetually louder. Eventually more crashes. Natalie pictured him just grabbing and throwing random items throughout the hotel room. She guessed it was the soap and shampoo bottles that landed against the wall. The ice tray and glasses took a tumble across the carpet. She felt bad for hotel housekeeping—all the random disgusting messes they had to clean up. And it was never their fault that things got destroyed. It always went back to a truth as old as time—people suck.

Natalie decided she had heard enough. Time to kindly request that this guy stop ruining her Zen. She went out to the hall and knocked on his door, room 420. The yelling stopped; she heard footsteps toward the door. A man in his forties opened the door. He stood over six feet, strongly built. He had light brown hair flowing off a chiseled face. She could see how, on a good day, he was extremely attractive. Right now, his face was slightly red and crinkled from a fit of rage. She guessed his current blood pressure to be about three times the normal amount. His rosy, angry complexion extended down the front of his unbuttoned shirt. He glared at her with dark brown eyes.

Before he could speak, Natalie said, "I am trying to relax next door. Could you calm down? Or maybe move to a different room?"

His response took her off guard. This was not a man accustomed to a woman being the lead in a confrontation. "I'm sorry, just trying to deal with some shit here."

She looked at him. He rolled his head toward his phone and started shaking his hand with it. "I lose my temper once on her, and she can't get over it. I mean, Jesus, is it that bad if you throw a punch one fucking time?"

Very rarely in her life could she remember a time when she

was perplexed by an answer. On one hand, he seemed to have genuine manners when answering the door; on the other, he was guilty of domestic abuse.

The physician in Natalie took over. Her thought was to help this man. "I am staying next door to you. How about we have a drink?"

The man looked her up and down, pretending to weigh his options. Realistically, he only considered his blind luck in this matter. "Fuck yeah. Let me make another call, and I'll be over."

Natalie backed away, heading toward her room. She took off her coat, grabbed some small change, and headed to the vending machines. He seemed like a rum and Coke kind of guy. She took two Cokes out of the vending machine and a water for herself.

Ten minutes later, the man was at her door. She welcomed him in and opened up the fridge, revealing a row of miniature drinks. She grabbed the two Jack Daniels and a Ketel One. While he kept talking in apologies and explanations, she poured drinks. "I understand," she responded, not actually taking note of what he had said for the last two minutes. She handed him a full glass of Coke with two mini bottles worth of the jack in it. He guzzled it down in quick fashion.

She was taken aback at how quickly his tone changed. "I told her so many times, and we keep going over the same shit. It's not my fault she pisses me off so bad."

Natalie continued to nod, anxious to help the man. He was clearly struggling with his anger and wanted to make his marriage work. "Let me ask you. Do you love her? And follow-up question. How often do you show it?"

He looked at her, confused for a moment, striking a more than necessary pose before answering. "Yeah, sure I love her. But sometimes I fall, ya know. I don't mean to do it, but a man has needs. God says to forgive thy neighbor." He looked at Natalie as though he had just reinvented the wheel with his wisdom. "And a woman needs to know her place sometimes. Yeah, she handles the kids. But who keeps a roof over their heads?" He smiled at Natalie and sucked down the rest of the drink.

"Do you think maybe she has dreams other than being a housewife?" she asked.

He took the liberty of going to the mini bar and taking out one of the Heinekens. "Got a bottle opener?"

Natalie went over to the sink area and grabbed a bottle opener from the drawer. Natalie continued, "Or maybe she doesn't want you to view it as a chore but, rather, your responsibility as a parent?"

He grabbed the beer from her. "Well maybe," he began "You women should be grateful we stick around. So many of you just can't handle kids and a job. Suck it the fuck up like the rest of us, ya know." He smiled at her as he took a long pull from the bottle.

Suddenly, he could not breathe. He tasted beer in his mouth without air; his throat was locked. He dropped the bottle, grabbing for his neck. He sucked at the air like a newborn on its mother. Nothing, no air came as panic set into his face. He felt Natalie's hand gripped around something. He tried to pull away. That only made it worse. He coughed and spit, trying to breathe. The pain was escalating into his brain. Natalie stood firm, one hand around her drink, the other holding onto the bottle opener. She sent the corkscrew straight through his trachea. She held him by the neck, yanking him in different directions gasping for air. *The pain*, she thought, *must be overwhelming.* She led him closer to the sink, above which was a collection of cooking knives. Natalie calmly set her drink down on the counter. Although he was clearer the stronger of the two, he was afraid to make any sudden movements. Natalie knew very well that he was in a precarious situation. It would take less force than opening a beer bottle to yank his entire throat open. She grabbed a long knife with a serrated edge. His eyes grew wide with shock at the sight of the knife. The good-looking man's hands did not know what to do.

In that second, he could not decide whether to keep pulling on the corkscrew or defend himself from the shiny blade. With her right arm, she thrusted at an upward angle directly into his balls. Her left hand pulled hard on the corkscrew, dislocating his trachea from the back of his larynx. The blade had never been used before. It cut through testicle as though it was butter. A guttural scream came from his mouth. With one hand he tried to pull on the corkscrew; the other he went to protect his manhood. Natalie was overjoyed with the picture of a gaping slice right up into his body.

Still standing without any air, he was powerless to stop what came next. His face went from a rosy red to a dark purple. The color change reminded her of Barney the dinosaur, his little useless Tyrannosaurus rex hands waving in the air. Natalie sawed through his testicles directly into his dick. Then she slowly withdrew the blade. Tears flowed down his cheeks. Screaming was choked off by bloody bubbles out of his mouth. He fought with her hands, at the same time turning ashen gray. He slowly sank to the floor, bleeding out and choking at the same time. Blood, vomit, and water poured from his mouth. A minute went by until he dropped completely, nearly motionless, still moaning. He lay on the floor, eyes pleading with her. She let go of the bottle opener and backed away, allowing him to die on his own. He was still wiggling behind her while she washed her hands.

Natalie was slightly annoyed at herself for making such an impromptu decision. She had time to prepare herself and the room for what was to come. She picked up the Heineken and smashed it into the side of her head. Breaking a beer bottle is not as easy as we have been told. It took three good smacks to break it. Next, she went into the bathroom. Natalie took a deep breath. She took three steps and threw her entire body headfirst through the glass shower door.

28

FATE

The call came in as a homicide stemming from a domestic dispute. It was a typical scene pulling up. All three emergency squads were surrounding the parking lot—fire trucks flanking the sides and in between two ambulances, cop cars of all labels scattered among them. Frank stepped out at the front entrance at the hotel. The first thing he noticed was the slender woman in her midthirties covered in blood and shiny spots he assumed was glass. The medics were picking her over as uniformed officers interviewed her. Frank went inside following the row of investigators to the room in question. *Holy shit* was his internal response upon entering. The man had been carved from tip to stern.

"Detective." A response from one of the local cops. The young officer in uniform approached Frank with a notebook in hand.

"Walk me through it," Frank responded.

"According to the woman's account, she met the guy in

the hallway. He was staying in the adjoining room. They hit it off. He comes over for a drink. After a couple, he got touchy. She was not into it. It got nasty. He smashed the bottle over her head and threw her through the shower door. She says she kept the bottle opener in her hand the whole time after he started beating on her. She wakes up and he is assaulting her on the floor. She puts the corkscrew in his throat. His pants were already down so she grabs the knife—end of story. The victim is forty-seven, two prior arrests for domestic battery; his name is Ronald Dumpt."

Frank took a good look around the room. Pictures and evidence were still in the process of being collected. At this point, there was no reason to suspect anything other than a defensive assault case turned homicide. He spent about thirty minutes going through the room piece by piece. He made his way downstairs to find the victim in this case.

She was a thirty-four-year-old critical care doctor. The first thing he noticed was her calm demeanor. Certainly, she was attractive in a simple way—not at all done up, little to no makeup. Her seeming indifference to the entire situation was what took him by surprise. "Hi, Natalie. The officer walked me through what happened inside. Can you elaborate at all? I do not want to upset you. I know this is a shock to the system, and you have had a hell of a day."

Natalie looked at him. "You should contact his wife. He was on the phone with her before we met. He mentioned her before he attacked me."

Frank wrote down notes on her response. "Did he say anything else? Also, can I ask why you were at the hotel?"

Natalie replied, "I'm in town for my father's funeral. This is an emotional time, and I am not sure how to process it. The guy did not say anything else. He had a drink and came at me swinging."

"Natalie, what is your last name?"

"Volos."

"OK, Natalie Volos. We are going to be in touch. But for right now, I want you to go with the medics, and they are going to give you a workup."

Frank left Natalie with the paramedics. Her relaxation could be attributed to shock, he thought. Something about her, though, really threw him off. She was pretending. After years of investigations, he could tell who was upset and who might be guiltier than they put on. *Caw! Caw!* The cry caught Frank's attention. He glanced back at the ambulance where Natalie Volos was being bandaged by the medics. On top of the ambulance sat half a dozen pitch-black crows. The only reason he even gave them a moment's notice was that they appeared to be looking right at him.

29

LIBRARY CARD

Christian had left the house faster than he'd originally planned. Seeing Lena was a reminder to him that he was not alone. A better brother would spend more time checking in on his sisters. He thought back to all those nights huddled together with the knife in his hand—he and Lena wide awake, waiting for something inevitably terrible to happen. Natalie was always in a daze. She was clearly scared. Sometimes her aloof nature seemed a good defense against terror. It was a safer place up in the clouds. She would sit calmly with her eyes closed, just waiting. Christian could not remember saying it out loud; he knew they'd had discussions about the monsters. They called them shadow people. He remembered the movie *Ghost*. In that movie, the bad people got taken to hell by dark figures that moved like cartoons. The shadow people were like that. You could be sitting or walking at night, when, suddenly, a part of the dark space moved toward you. Christian had broken their promise only one time. He had spent the night under his bed, after waking up unable to breathe. A pair of dark hands had wrapped around his nose and mouth. He'd felt an ice-like grip holding his head down into the pillow. He stared at the ceiling while he drowned. His consciousness began to fade. He heard three words in his left ear. "You smell funny."

That was the one time he told their mother something was not right. She looked him dead in the eye. "You're too old to fear monsters under your bed. Your sisters rely on you, so grow tougher."

He had even shown her the finger bruises around his throat.

That house only brought him back to terrible memories. Why had he even come back? Lena told him what their aunt had said. He struggled to believe it was anything but a cursed piece of concrete and siding. If he stayed miles away, these thoughts stayed away as well. On his way back to the turnpike, Christian passed Broadway Road. He knew about three miles down the road was the city library. He turned right onto Broadway and decided to do a little research he probably should have done years ago.

He took turns through the town he had not taken since he was a little kid. He walked into the library for the first time in twenty-five years at least. It was apparent the place had had a face-lift, but even that was a little tattered. The town itself was just trying to hold on. It was a collection of senior citizens once employed in blue-collar factory jobs, most likely associated with steel. The town lay north of Philadelphia and, seventy years prior, had produced all the steel needed by the allied forces to kill off Nazis. That same group that had fired guns made of the raw material had come home after the war and settled down. They'd found good union-supported jobs that offered a livable wage and a pension plan. The problem was that the era was long gone. Steel was shut down all together by the early nineties. Most of the city population now used government-funded loans to open small businesses. Much like the library, the town needed a serious face-lift.

No matter the weather elsewhere, there was a never-ending dark cloud hovering over this part of America. You could see it in the people. Their attitudes were always just a little harder. The lines in their faces formed deeper at a younger age. The world just beat them down before their time. Christian knew a great example of this worn population would be waiting for him inside. There was your typical library crowd scattered about. Some schoolkids gathered in the corner surrounded by teachers. Every other reading table had a person doing deep research. Upon closer inspection, he realized it was mostly homeless men taking a nap in a dry place. He ignored all of it and went straight to the information desk.

An older gray haired woman in her sixties smiled at him. "Yes, can I help you?"

Christian realized he didn't actually know what he was looking for. "This may sound a bit odd. I am trying to do research on my childhood home. My parents passed away, and we are putting the house on the market. The realtor we are using needs more information."

The lady smiled at him and said, "Absolutely. We assist with these things all the time. You will have to go to the hall of deeds. However, sometimes people want to look up historical facts during the time the homes were built. Would you be interested in that?" Her face perked upon asking the question.

"I definitely would," Christian replied.

He enjoyed watching her and seeing her eagerness to help. Clearly, the poor librarians anymore were disregarded as a resource—relics living in a digital world. There was anxiety building in his gut. The library seemed to have gotten darker.

As they passed through rows and shelves, he felt his mood change. He no longer felt curiosity but, instead, anger.

The nice librarian pointed him to the microfiche section—a collection of pictures taken from old newspaper articles. "We have every weekly paper going back before World War II. If it occurred in this area, this is where you can find a story about it."

Christian made himself at home there in the back of the library. This was his type of happy place. It was dark and quiet. For a while, he flipped through months and years, starting in the early '90s. It was fascinating to see the writing change. The wording used, even the printing styles shifted decade to decade. He skipped through year after year, following world-changing events at the local level—'80s, '70s, '60s.

He stopped at 1963. An article caught his eye. A World War II veteran was incarcerated after attempted murder of his wife. His name was Leonard Volos. Her name was Greta. Leonard had displayed disturbing behavior prior to his arrest outside of their home on Derry Street. Greta had awoken to Leonard pouring gasoline on the children. Local doctors claimed he suffered from something yet identified but similar to sleepwalking. Christian skipped ahead by six months to a follow-up article. Leonard was released following a plea from his wife to the judge that he was not a harm to anyone. The judge agreed but ordered him to continue with psychiatric care for the following year. Christian didn't have to move ahead very far. Three weeks after Leonard had been released, there was another article about the death of a young couple with two children:

> Leonard and Greta Volos perished in an automobile accident north of Philadelphia while

out for a Sunday drive on March 22, 1963. They leave behind two children.

Witnesses say the car was found burning with the couple inside of it ten miles from their home on Derry Street. Police reports indicate that Greta was stuck by her necklace, which had become wrapped around the back of the passenger seat.

Leonard had apparently tried to help the poor trapped woman. His burnt body was found outside her door. Authorities believe he had been trying to open her door to help. That struck Christian as odd. How does a necklace get wrapped around a seat? In the fifties, there were no headrests—just a large seat now comparable to a living room couch.

There was a gritty black-and-white photo beneath the article. Christian strained to see the details. The car was charred black from front to back. In the passenger seat was a lump sticking out, also black; he had to assume that was his grandmother. He followed the photo, and outside her door was the strangest thing. Was that a hand? He was sure of it that was a hand on the door handle. It was bent at the wrist, the arm descended to the ground. The entire arm was burnt through. The body rested against the steel door frame blackened from top to bottom. Loose articles of clothing hung from the chest. White teeth stuck out of burned gums. The eye sockets empty black holes. He read the caption above again. "Local veteran dies trying to save wife."

Christian looked closely again. What if he wasn't trying to open the door? What if he was keeping it shut?

30

UNWELCOME

Lena drove up the turnpike, her head doing somersaults of frustration and curiosity. What did her aunt mean? Why did this even bother her? She had given up on knowing the past long ago. She had only gone to her aunt's house once in her life. She had been twelve or thirteen. Her mom had gone there desperate to speak to Mida. Lena had been told to stay in the car while her mom went inside. They were only there for probably thirty minutes. Lena remembered spending the whole time memorizing every single part of the neighborhood—the dilapidated barn on the corner, how many turns off the highway it had taken. She recalled every street sign and lamppost. Lena sped off the turnpike, down Hamilton Street in what used to be a not-so-bad part of the city. Now most blocks had been left to ruin. Ivy hung on the sides of decaying brick. Wrought iron bars could be seen through windowless openings. She drove for ten minutes until the faded green sign caught her eye. Written in cracked white paint was Lazarus Street. One block in and second house on the left. That was it, she was 100 percent sure.

"OK, bitch, time for some fucking closure," she swore as she hopped out of the car.

She marched straight through the yellow dead grass, bypassing the walkway. She knew what would happen if she didn't get answers. This woman had no idea what she was capable of. She had raised her right hand, ready to bring a thunderous strike on the door, when the door opened. There in the dark stood the tall, lean woman she knew as Aunt Mida. The woman cocked her head to the side and smiled a peculiar smile. She had a mouthful of yellow tarnished teeth. Her skin was so pale you would think she had never seen the sun. There were small sores or cuts on her face. In public, her skin complexion would scare people away. Her stance in the doorway was strong.

"You're finally here," her aunt seethed. "Do you want to come in?"

Lena had felt so bold ten seconds before this encounter. It felt as though her knees collapsed under her. She stood unsteady. "No. Answer me here."

Mida took a long look out into the street over Lena's shoulder. "What would you like to know?" her aunt asked, still with a crooked smile.

"What did you mean when you said it wasn't the house?"

Her aunt looked at her with pity. "I meant just that you kids grew up in a haunted place. It wasn't the house haunting you."

Lena stared at her, indicating she needed more.

"It may be difficult for you to go back that far in your mind. I promise, if you do, you will not like what is there."

Now Lena was annoyed. She had no tolerance for games—especially a game from a woman she didn't know. Somehow, her aunt thought she could speak to Lena like they had a telepathic connection.

"When your father and I were children, we felt the same thing. The walls in that house moved. I saw the cloud several times. It told your father things. Did you ever see the cloud?" her aunt hissed with that last word, emphasizing the gravity of it. Her eyes drifted above Lena, looking beyond. "I was so scared all the time," she said.

"Scared of the house?" Lena asked in a pleading fashion.

"Scared of the people," her aunt replied. Her aunt's eyes came back to Lena.

"What people?" Lena asked.

Mida looked at her strongly once again. "The dead people." Aunt Mida smacked her lips. "The Indians warned our parents, warned the builders, warned everyone. But no one listened."

A feeling of sheer terror overtook Lena. She remembered the Indian from childhood. He appeared in her mind clear as day, where a moment before, there had been a blank space in time. She couldn't leave now when she was so close to answers she had wanted since childhood. The look on her aunt's face took all that need away. Lena had drifted off in her thoughts. Now her aunt stood much closer to her. "You should leave now. I don't like you."

Lena backed away, breathless. She didn't turn her back until she had reached the car. Her aunt stared at her from the doorway until Lena drove off with white knuckles.

31

ONION LAYERS

Frank had been going over the interview questions asked to Ms. Natalie Volos after the murder of a man in her hotel room. He had dug deeper into her past, and some interesting things had popped up. She had gone to college at Temple med school at UPenn and then taken a residency in, of all places, Montana. Frank had been to Montana and could understand the natural tranquility that lived there. However, the woman he met was not a person looking for time with nature. She seemed much more calculated than that. She had worked at Central Montana Health Center. Not only had she headed to the boondocks; she had taken a job at a no-name hospital. Why not a Cedar Sinai or a Hopkins? It struck him as somewhat odd that someone with her talent had settled for less than. She had gone to high school at St. Johns in the Kensington area of Philadelphia. Prior to that, her middle school was also in northeast Philadelphia. The coincidence hit Frank like a sledgehammer. She had gone to St. Catherine's.

Frank could not get home fast enough. They'd all gone to the same school—his victims and now this doctor involved in a brutal homicide. It was an impossibility this was purely coincidence, right? He pulled into the driveway and jumped out of the car with his file. Once inside, he poured through all known victim's records. There, in front of him, all had attended the same school. He was about to declare victory before noticing the date of birth on Natalie Volos's driver's license. There was a two- to four-year gap between their ages. She might have met the victims. They were all older than her but that doesn't mean she didn't know them. So maybe this was purely coincidence. "No fucking way," Frank said aloud. He became keenly aware that desperation had gotten the better of him. He pulled up the other curious murders over the past decade. All victims were the same ages. He went year by year—1995 St. Catherine alumni, 1999 St. Catherine alumni, and 2001 St. Catherine alumni. These people had gone to middle school and junior high together.

Hours ticked by alone in the garage. On his computer was a google search for Natalie Volos. Next to the computer, a collection of photographs taken today at the crime scene. There was some basic information right off the bat about her graduate details, medical certifications, and so on. There were articles about critical care progression and patient rights to die. She had written extensively in medical journals about the benefits of palliative care during long illnesses. There was little to nothing about her personal life.

He was debating on which link about her to click on next when he noticed something way at the bottom of the search page. She had mentioned that she was in town for her father's funeral. "Michael Volos died Sunday after a long illness. He leaves behind a sister and three children." The obituary had no other personal details. It was a generic write-up the papers had to do when notified of a death. It was enough to tell Frank that Natalie had siblings.

Frank called the home where Michael Volos had lived. According to his driver's license information, it was a house north of the city. He tried to call several times. The line had been disconnected. He put in a call to the local phone company. The line to that house had been disconnected for at least five years. Obviously, Michael had been living somewhere without human interaction. Frank called the funeral home listed under the obituary column online. The funeral director informed him Michael had been taken from a long-term care facility for dementia patients.

A woman answered on the second ring. "This is Tulip Nursing Facility. What do you want?"

Frank was already annoyed at her tone but reminded himself what the mission here was. "I am calling about a Michael Volos who was living in your facility."

The woman gave him a hard time about HIPAA law violations—not that she knew what it meant only that she didn't want to be bothered. That was until he said, "I am a detective with the Philadelphia Police. Put a manager on the phone immediately."

After speaking to the much more personable manager, Frank had derived three things. The first was that Michael Volos had no visitors except his sister in the five years that he was at the nursing facility. Second, his three children had not once called or tried to see him. And third, the circumstances around his placement at the facility were extremely suspicious. Five years ago, his wife had been found dead in the front yard of their home. Neighbors had come outside at 3:00 a.m. to find her on fire. A can of gasoline was next to her, along with a lighter in her hand. Michael Volos had been found in the basement by himself, standing in the center of the room. He'd never spoken a word to detectives. As far as anyone knew, he never spoke again. No one at the facility had ever heard him. His sister had come only the one time. Eyewitness reports said they'd sat in silence for two hours staring at each other.

Frank asked if it was possible to see any security footage from the one visit that Michael Volos had received. The manager let him know that all the patients had to be monitored on a twenty-four-hour basis according to state laws, since they were susceptible to abuse or neglect. The manager had the tapes on file; he agreed to email Frank what he had.

32

STRANGER DANGER

Natalie could not help but think what a strange thing fate could be. Meeting the detective had made her think of the reason she'd moved back to Philadelphia in the first place. In her mind, she knew it was always meant to be. Not long after the end of her residency, she had encountered a true twist of fate. She was working a day shift in the ICU just trying to get through the day. An elderly man in his early seventies had come into the hospital for advanced COPD. He was now admitted to the ICU because his breathing had become so bad. She did not expect him to survive the night. He had written a will declaring he did not want life-saving measures taken. There was a note stating the man was easily confused and had a history of psychiatric problems. A nurse from his assisted living facility had come with him. No family was listed under next of kin. Natalie entered the room to find a fairly ordinary scene. The old man sat in silence with his eyes closed. His face was covered in dark brown moles. He had been recently given a shave. It was a hack job. There were little patches of gray hair on his neck. Small cuts and bruising lined his cheek bones. Long white hair hung over his ears. The visiting nurse sat in the corner on her phone.

"Hi, Mr. Allon. I am the doctor covering the ICU. I just wanted to check on you to see how you are doing."

The man made no movement of any kind. He didn't even open his eyes. His head remained bent forward to his chest.

The nurse in the corner spoke up. "He doesn't ever talk. At the home, we go about our business. Sometimes he'll grunt or something, but that's really it."

Natalie hoped to gather more information about the patient's state of mind. "Well, we're keeping him on oxygen for the time being. His oxygen saturation is slowly dropping, so I want to make sure he understands what is happening."

The nurse just gave a shrug and a look to say she didn't know what else to tell her. "He doesn't have any family. The place he came from was a state psychiatric ward."

Natalie looked at the man feeling somewhat helpless. "OK, well, Mr. Allon, if you need anything or have questions about your care, I want you to talk to me. My name is Dr. Natalie Volos."

Natalie had turned to leave when a scream behind her took over the room. "Volos," the old man yelled.

Natalie spun. The old man now sat head up with eyes wide open—drilling a hole through her face. The man motioned with a finger for her to come near him. Natalie stepped forward. She saw the nurse in the corner also watching the scene unfold.

"Michael," he said.

She looked at him with a pondering look. "My father's name is Michael." Natalie fell deep with curiosity.

"Orphan." The man coughed.

"Yes, he was an orphan, as well as my mother."

The man gasped, eyes growing larger. He began to choke and sputter.

"Calm down, Mr. Allon. Catch your breath."

The old man's right hand shot up, grabbing ahold of Natalie's scrub top. He pulled with miraculous strength. She was now an inch from his face, trying to remain calm. He pulled her ear to his mouth. "Evil boy and slave girl." The man released her and began violently coughing. Blood poured from his lips, and his eyes grew red.

Natalie called for help outside the room. He died only an hour later, suffocating on his own lung fluids.

Natalie had never been one to dwell. She had done so well in medical school for that very reason. The amount of information coming at you was overwhelming by superhero standards. She was able to dissect what she needed and completely void herself of nonpertinent information—not that any part of medicine should be considered unimportant. When you needed to pass a test on vascular pathophysiology, it was best not to be worried about the previous test on bedside mannerisms. With all that skill, why couldn't she put Mr. Allon's last words out of her mind? She had waited two full weeks before giving in to curiosity. She started with Mr. Allon's former nursing home. It was a home run by the state in the middle of South Philadelphia. She called, explaining to the shift supervisor that she had been his doctor prior to his passing. She was simply trying to find out if he did, in fact, have family he was unaware of. The supervisor was happy to assist.

His full name was Charles Allon. Born in New Jersey, he'd been given to the state at the age of twelve. He had been a foster child until eighteen. Natalie had to push further and ask if his foster facilities were listed in his records. He had lived in three facilities but only one for the majority of his adolescent years. It was a private foster home in Fishtown, a small section of eastern Philadelphia. The home was listed as belonging to Kathy McConnell and Walter McConnell. Natalie got the address and made her way over. The rain seemed to pick up as she neared the watery area of the city. Fishtown was named aptly, as it resided next to the harbor. It had become a much nicer and more affordable section of the city to live over the last decade. Prior to that, it had been a haven for rotting naval ships and fish-processing plants.

Natalie pulled up to 46 Norris Street. Unlike the rest of the rising neighborhood, this house looked as though everyone was hoarding their trash in it. The front yard was littered with cans, bags, random pieces of an air-conditioning unit from what she could tell. What used to be a lovely three-story colonial now was a dilapidated garbage heap. Natalie was afraid that the former foster home tenants may still live here. The place should only house rodents, not people. On second thought, which one was more disgusting? The thought made her smile.

She walked up to the front screen door as it waved back and forth, smacking the wood paneling of the frame. Behind it, the front door was either open or not there anymore. Natalie took a hard look into the dark void of a front entrance.

A man stepped forward, almost lunging at her from behind the torn screen. "Well, hello, young lady?" he said with a yellow smile from ear to ear.

Where the hell did he come from? she thought. "Hi. Is this the former foster home owned by the McConnells?"

The man looked startled. Natalie could see he was wearing large black combat boots with the shoelaces undone. His T-shirt, also black, with holes showing reddish skin underneath, blanketed the front and sides. The part she wanted to avoid was the undercarriage. She did not need keen eyes to notice the man had jean shorts on so tight they were hugging his genitals. "Why yes, it is. No one has asked about the McConnells for years. Let me guess. You used to live in this lovely establishment?"

Natalie noticed, for the first time, he was wearing a thick shade of purple lipstick. Taking in his entire portrait, the man was truly terrifying. "No. I am wondering about two people who lived here a long time ago, over forty years. There's no chance you would have been around."

The man smiled again. "Why yes. I was here. My mother and father ran this place. I was their one and only real baby boy. Of course, you would never know it. They spent all their time worrying about the other kids who showed up—the poor dears. I only hope the children who passed through here are grateful for the sacrifices my family made." He finished this with a long sigh.

"Are your parents still around?" Natalie followed.

The man took a long look at the roof above him. "Well, one could make the argument they are around. Of course, you could even argue they are just up and down." He chuckled at his little joke, making the moment extremely unsettling for Natalie.

She decided this man was dangerous; get to the point. "I am wondering about a man named Michael Volos and a girl named Valerie. Do you or your parents know anything about them?"

The man stopped playing with his fingernails. He stared through the screen at Natalie. The look he had reminded her of a cat waiting to pounce on a mouse leaving its hole. She instinctively balled her car keys in her hand with the largest starter key sticking out. If he came through that screen, the key was going in his eye. "Michael was here for a *verrrrrrry* long time. Valerie followed him like a dog. The two of them never left each other. They played with me all the time. They all played with me." The man's teeth gritted. Natalie was pretty sure she may have heard a molar crack.

"Who is all?" she asked.

He stuck a dirty index finger into his mouth. The finger came out with a pop from the cheek. "Michael was a dangerous little boy. He liked to play tricks on people. He, Valerie, and Mida, always playing games.

Natalie perked up at this. "Mida. Was Mida here also?"

The man started to cry a little. "They said they would take me with them when they left. But they didn't. They all just left me here. We played so many tricks on all the kids. Michael wanted to make them crazy. Michael said the Indian said he would make crazy people." The man began blubbering. "Michael wanted to go back to the house. The house had the funny demons under it. They gave him powers. They all had powers but not me." The man was weeping loudly.

Natalie dropped her guard a bit trying to take this in. "What are you talking about? What powers and what funny demons?"

The man attempted to compose himself. "Michael said his daddy was bad because he moved into the house. The Indian told Michael his daddy was weak. Michael said he had the power to do whatever he wanted."

Natalie accepted she may not get exact answers at this point. The cryptic nature of the conversation left her trying to pry for more. "What was his daddy supposed to do? What couldn't he do that Michael was supposed to?"

The man in the jean thong scratched his cheek so hard blood began to poor from under a mole. He wiped blood from the wound on his bottom lip. "Kill all of us," he said. The man muttered something Natalie could not make out.

It pushed her patience. "I'd like to understand what you're saying. Can you explain it to me, please?"

"It's pretty simple stuff, little lady. Michael said him and Valerie would make little demons." His focus returned to Natalie. "Did they do it?"

Natalie stared at him, unsure how to respond. "You mean did they have children?"

A smile crossed his face. He looked away and began walking back into the house. "You run along now, sweetie. I'm starting to feel a little nibbly."

Natalie backed away toward her car. Sitting atop her car were three black crows. Water bounced off their feathers, making its way to the ground. The three made no movement the closer she got. Natalie stood still, watching them as they watched her.

The rain picked up intensity. Through the storm she heard it. "The dead in the dark are alive in the light."

Her head whipped around to the man poking his head out of the top floor window. He blew her a kiss. She turned back to find the three strangers had gone.

33

MISS SUNSHINE

The house stood still feeling the summer wind knock on its siding. The children had been back and then left in such a hurry. Wasn't it a good house? Their childhood had had some pitfalls. That wasn't its fault.

He crept up so fast not even the grass noticed the stranger staring from the road. There he stood, a man who had been here before. He still wore that long silver braid. His skin was ever more creased and cracked. The eyes were as remembered, dark like the moon. He stared at the house, so the house stared back. The breeze came through the holly trees right between them. The man spoke without moving his lips. The house could hear his words. "Are you scared of being alone?"

The house listened without answering.

"When their wicked deeds are done, you will be." The old Indian turned his head to the left looking at a small patch of yard just next to the corner of the house. A memory in time came into view for him.

The house remembered it as well.

The day is dark, the grass is trimmed. There is a little girl with blue overalls and a red ribbon in her hair. She is playing quietly by herself. Lena is ten years old. She is outside on the front yard. She has created dolls with sticks. The sticks are decorated in leaves and grass. She has named these makeshift toys Mickey and Minnie.

"Minnie, I am home from work. How are the kids?"

"Oh, Mickey, I'm so glad to see you, I've prepared something so special for you!"

"Well what is it, Minnie, my sweet?"

And with that, Lena breaks the stick legs of Mickey. "Ah, Minnie, what did you do? *Ahahahah* it hurts, Minnie. I need a doctor!"

Lena reaches behind her, where she has a red balloon in the grass. The balloon is filled almost halfway with something heavier than just air. Lena unties the knot she fashioned into it. She begins to pour the liquid onto her Mickey stick.

"Minnie, what are you doing? Cough, cough."

Lena goes into her right pocket where she has something hidden. "I told you, Mickey, my love, I have something special for you."

Lena now has a yellow lighter in her hand. She flicks it on. The stick catches fire immediately,

"Ah, Minnie, ah it burns!"

Suddenly there is a boot stomping on her doll. Lena looks up with anger rather than surprise. She stares up at the large dark-skinned man. His silver and black hair falls over his eyes.

"What are you doing, little one?"

Lena replies in a calm manner, "Practicing."

The man continues to look down at her. "Little white princess, you will charm all the Mickeys you meet. You must be careful not to get greedy. Greed is within you, and it will undo you."

"But how will I get what I want?" she asks.

The old man smiles. "Your people always get what they want." He stops to look up. The gaping smile stretches across his face. He looks to the sky and closes his eyes. The man chuckles.

Behind Lena in the bush a dark cloud idles.

"What is so funny?" Lena asks.

The old man brings his attention back to her. His eyes have grown darker and wider. Bright teeth are shown. His face begins to transform from man to woman under the waving hair. "You will give your people what they deserve."

"Mother, Father is telling the little girl what she will be become."

"Yes, my child."

"Do you miss him, Mother?"

"Yes, my child. But he will join us when the work is done."

34

WEIRDOS

To Frank's surprise, his inbox flashed within a couple of days. The manager was either bored or extremely diligent. Although Frank couldn't say so, he was really appreciative. Going through all those visitor logs must have been a painstaking process. The file was dated March 22, 2009. The video was a little grainy but overall of decent quality.

Michael was sitting on the side of his bed hunched forward. He looked like a small man, not over five foot six. He was thin but not sickly. He was wearing a white and green gown. The pants were the same color, with a candy cane pattern wrapping around them. The bed was a solid white mattress held within a shiny metal bedframe. A woman entered the room from outside the camera's view. Frank assumed the door was just out of the camera's range.

He realized there was audio on the file because he could hear her footsteps. He turned the microphone on his computer all the way up.

The woman was tall with thin shoulders. She was wearing a skirt and suit jacket. Her hair was pulled back very tightly. Her outfit looked old, very old. She reminded him of a German woman from the 1940s. She sat in the chair that had been left next to the bed. The two of them stared at each other without speaking for minutes. It was difficult to see her features from the camera angle. Her cheekbones were high with a tight facial structure. Her eyebrows appeared dark. There were many creases along the right side of her brow. They ran deep enough to resemble scarring.

Michael and his visitor made no movements. This continued for so long that Frank thought maybe the tape was frozen. Then Michael's head dropped down. Did he say something?

Frank made sure the volume was all the way up. He rewound just five seconds. He was sure Michael said something. "You left ..."

Frank rewound again, this time grabbing his headphones from the dresser. He plugged them into the computer and pressed them to his ears. "You left but ..."

Frank lowered his head, facing his feet under him. He hit the fifteen second replay button.

"You left but ..."

He hit the button again and again. He focused every sense into his ears.

"You left Buttersworth."

What the hell did that mean? You left Buttersworth? He was so confused, facing the floor, still trying to absorb this strange sentence. When he looked up, he screamed, flying backward over his chair onto the floor. The woman was in the camera. His heart was jumping so fast he might explode from the inside out. She was smiling a crooked smile with her head tilted. Her face was occupying the entire video space. Frank had no doubt in his logical mind, she was looking at him.

Frank had to take a moment to collect himself after turning the video off. "What the fuck was that?" he uttered aloud. "You're being crazy, Frank. Pull it together, man."

Frank sat at his table with a drink in hand. His mind rolled the information over. His heart was having difficulty normalizing. The father was left to ruin, and the mother was probably clinically insane. Now he knew that Natalie's mommy, daddy, and aunty were all out of their minds. That could explain her somber tone after a traumatic event. It didn't mean she is guilty of anything.

Going back to the school grudge idea, she was younger than the victims. However, she had siblings. Was there anything of interest there? The next oldest sister was closer in age to the victims. She had recently been married, according to a post he'd found. It was a website called The Knot; it showed a picture of the attractive couple. The groom was clearly her elder by a decade or more. Unlike her younger sister, this one, named Lena, seemed to appreciate a nicer living style. It was apparent from the rock on her finger. There were a plethora of photos from island vacations. Once again, scrolling further down, he found an obituary article on a previous husband. Further down than that was another article of a poor nineteen-year-old Lena who'd survived an apartment fire but had tragically lost her boyfriend. Lena Volos seemed to have a lifelong run of tragedy. He kept going out of pure curiosity at this point.

On page three of his google search, he saw a strange article. It was dated from 1999. There was a picture attached to it of a high school kid and his girlfriend. In the picture was an attractive blond girl. She was no older than seventeen. It appeared she had survived a car accident that had killed her boyfriend. He went line by line, not wanting to miss any of the details in the short article. The boy had been a football player at Haverford high school. How does a seventeen-year-old football jock wind up dead on the Pacific Coast Highway in California? His eyes darted back to the picture at the top of the article. That girl was no innocent cheerleader. She was poison, and this kid was her first.

Frank stepped back from his computer and ran his hands through his thinning hair. He closed his eyes to block out distraction. He needed to focus, because this all was clearly connected. He cleared the checks of Mom and Dad. Natalie was involved in a brutal hotel homicide if not more. Now that he had seen the parents and learned of the sister, he started to wonder what other incidents Natalie was involved in. Lena was the older sister, whose male partners were destined for a short life.

Only the brother was left. He was two years older than Lena, which put him at the same age as the victims. The brother's name was Christian. It was mentioned in the obituary for Michael Volos. There were no photos included. He googled the name Christian Volos. Nothing, absolutely nothing came up under a search. This man had no social media accounts of any kind. He had no certifications listed. His background check came back with only a driver's license number and photo. He appeared to be a serious-looking guy in his thirties. Frank knew not to judge someone by a driver's license picture. If anyone had really noticed Frank's, they would have thought him to be a criminal, not a cop. No criminal background, no posted media; the only thing was a background check requested by a private security company. Frank knew these companies were very protective of their clients. It was easy to obtain someone's personal information if they gave anything away. No security company in the world wanted to be the ironic poster child of a stolen identity case.

Frank called. About an hour later a supervisor agreed to give him the name of the company requesting the check. It was the Philadelphia Zoo security office.

35

CATHOLIC GUILT

The zoo security supervisor did not have one negative thing to say about Christian Volos. The man never mentioned family and rarely spoke of his social life. The security office viewed him as a perfect employee. That was enough to make Frank suspicious. He had learned on the job that people with the most to hide were very good at hiding it.

After the call, he drove north. Here he sat once again in the rain behind St. Catherine's Church. The school was the connection between this family and his victims. Frank looked up through the pelted windshield. On the top of the rock face in the rear of the church were small carved gargoyle creatures of every kind. The craftmanship was exquisite, he thought. Typical of the Roman Catholics, he thought, stone monsters portraying fear. He followed a brick covered walkway into the back of the church also labeled "School Entrance."

He walked inside, struck by how dimly lit the place was. There was that incense smell attacking his nostrils. It was a type of incense only found in churches. He had spent his time at parties during the seventies; he knew incense. This was a strong potpourri, like a perfume. He followed the lighting to a front office.

In the front sat a small gray-haired woman. "Can I help you, sir?" she asked with a wide smile under thick brown glasses.

"Yes, I hope so. My name is Frank, and I'm doing a little research for the Philadelphia Police Department. It involves some students who went here years ago."

The woman perked up. "Well of course. How can we help?"

Frank did not want to make this official, for fear it would backfire into the wrong channels. He decided subtlety was the correct approach. "I have a few names, and I was hoping someone could tell me more about them. They went here many years ago. So I understand if it is not possible. I am just taking a shot in the dark."

The woman looked at him affectionately, reaching to the phone on her right. "I have the person for you," she said.

Frank stood in the hallway admiring the trophy case collecting dust on the outer rim. He was startled back when a face was staring at him in the reflective mirror. He turned, embarrassed at his reaction.

A warm smile greeted him. "Hello. I am sorry to have surprised you. As we get older, for some reason, we also get scarier."

Frank found the woman's remark very humorous, albeit dry. He guesstimated her age to be in the early eighties, and she was wearing a traditional nun outfit.

"I am Sister Teresa." She was small in stature. He would be shocked if she cleared five foot.

"That's no problem at all, Sister. As we cops get older, I guess we get more sheepish."

They both stood in silence for a moment, enjoying the lighthearted introduction.

"My name is Frank King. I'm a detective with the Philadelphia Police Department. I do have some questions. However, I must ask you to keep it between us if that is OK? If not, I completely understand."

The nun looked at him with a warm smile. "Detective, at my age, I am happy to have any conversation with anyone who comes through the door. How can I help you?"

She turned and began walking the length of the hall. Frank followed, preparing his words carefully, not really paying attention to their direction. "The nice woman at the front desk told me you have been here the longest. I hear you've made St. Catherine's home since the fifties."

She continued a slow walk, making a right down an adjoining hallway lined by golden and wood crucifixes. "I came here after my time at a smaller convent in Romania. It was my home only by birth. I never knew my own parents. I had been left on the doorstep of a convent with no note of any kind. The sisters raised me as their own. This world is all I have ever known.

"Oddly enough, through this work, I have become part of many worlds. I have lived many lives in knowing these children and seeing them grow over the decades. I have seen the city grow as well, which I believe you can probably relate to."

Frank smiled while continuing the slow stroll. He liked this nun. "Yes, Sister. Unfortunately the majority of lives I have been a part of are those of the deceased. This is the line of work I chose. I don't regret it, but sometimes I wonder what a different choice would have done." Frank shook his head, wondering why he felt the need to say such a thing. He wished sometimes that he could not have such a cynical view.

"Only the strongest can carry the burden of all us sinners and our mistakes."

Frank stopped in his tracks. He looked over at the little nun. She stood, still smiling at him.

After a second of silence and warm reflection, they continued to walk. The hallway now crossed under a spiraling wooden stairwell. He could tell from the change in flooring and tile they were now entering a different building connected to the church. "Sister, over the last several years, your former students have turned up in our case files. I am not saying they were criminals; all evidence points to the opposite. However, and I am sorry to tell you this, they were murdered."

The nun kept walking at her pace with her head bowed slightly, making no response.

"With all honesty, sister, they were killed brutally. Their cases have gone under the radar because of jurisdictions and other things. I have made the only connection that I am aware of."

The nun stopped walking now and faced the detective.

"Sister, they all went to this school and would've been here together. I know it sounds like a stretch, but I am wondering if this goes back to a long-held grudge by another student."

The woman stared at him for several moments before raising her hand to urge him to continue their walk.

Her silence was confusing Frank. He wondered if maybe he had upset her. "I am not trying to upset you in any way. I know you must see these kids as your own in a certain way."

She took a long breath, closing her eyes for a moment. She spoke more forcefully than he had anticipated. "You are correct in saying they are mine; or at least they were my children in their formative years. What happens after that, I take no responsibility for. The truth, Detective, is that you do the best you can. It is nature versus nurture. Many of these children came in here as little angels. We can always tell who are beyond our help. They will grow into the person we may or may not like regardless of our efforts. Can I assume these former students were in the same age range? I would guess in their mid to late thirties."

"Yes," Frank replied. He was unable to hide the shock in his voice at her accuracy. Her pace had quickened just a bit but noticeably.

They moved through a door labeled "Exit." Together they went down several flights of steps. Frank had to assume they were now in the basement under the old school. It was extremely dark with a thick, musty smell. Files and boxes littered every inch of flooring. The old woman moved steadily, dragging her fingers along the shelves as they passed.

Frank decided to push further. "The person who did these things, if in fact it really is one person, would be a male of the same age. He would be strong, probably in both mind and body, not to be too dramatic. These things took a tight constitution to execute. My guess is he would have been a loner but not unliked. Sister, is there anyone who comes to mind?"

Frank had been so worried about his words that he'd barely noticed they had stopped walking and were now crammed into a very tight row of Manila folders and cardboard boxes. Labels of all kinds were hung from the metal shelves. The boxes had worn names scrolled across them. On the floor were tabs of paper that had fallen off when the tape finally dried up.

Sister Teresa faced him now with a stern look in her eyes. With her left hand, she pointed to a small metal box. He followed her gaze. Tucked between the papers and pictures was an old lunch box—a metal one, worn all around.

His heart skipped a beat, giving him a mild panic attack. On the front facing him, in black marker were the initials "CV."

36

BACK TO THE BEGINNING

Christian had spent the day meticulously going through the old photographs and articles dating back to the '50s. He had assembled a family time line, which felt very odd, considering it was his family. In 1960, his grandfather and grandmother had moved into the house on Derry Street. Their names were Leonard and Greta. Leonard had a history of mental problems stemming back before the war. Greta seemed liked a run-of-the mill 1950's housewife. They had two children, his father Michael and his aunt Mida. In 1962, Leonard was put into a mental institution but released on the grounds that he follow court-ordered psychiatric evaluations. In 1963 both Leonard and Greta were killed in a car accident.

It was a very strange feeling to read newspaper clippings about the untimely death of his grandparents. He had never given them much thought because he'd never known them. He'd also never given thought to Mida. Their whole world only revolved around himself, Natalie, Lena, and their parents.

He wondered if his mother had secrets related to family she'd never mentioned. As far has he knew, his mother, Valerie, was an orphan. She'd met Michael when they were both given to the same foster family as teenagers.

Christian took a moment to recall stories about his mother and father's past. After thirty seconds, he realized that never in his life had they mentioned their lives together in the foster home. Mida was only brought up occasionally and elicited a violent outburst from his father. The house was claimed by his father. Christian felt a ping of guilt for not checking in on his father after his mother died. He had heard about it on the news. Their family contained five adults, yet not one of them spoke to each other. Christian reminded himself that guilt was a wasted emotion. His time with this was about done. Now he knew the timeline, and he had seen Lena; it was time to move on.

He fumbled with the buttons on the machine, as he was not accustomed to it. Before closing out the last article, he accidentally hit the arrow pointing to the right. The newspaper shifted a little, bringing a small corner article into focus. It caught his eye because of the street sign posted in the background. The sign said "Derry St." Christian sat back down, bringing his face closer to the article and using the magnification button to zoom in. The still photo was a construction site being worked on. The house could be theirs from the angle against the street sign. But that was not what caught his eye. In the background, past the construction workers were protesters. They looked like protesters from the way they stood in a row across the street. There were no signs of any kind. It looked like they were just standing and watching. He could count a dozen people, all elderly. They stood hand in hand, most with their heads bowed. The black-and-white photo blended some of the image together. He couldn't make out faces.

However, the man on the end stood out the most. He stood straight with his head up. The man had a long beard nearly touching his waistline. He did hold something in his hands. Christian tried refocusing the camera lens. He face was an inch from the screen. The man held a piece of paper. "What is dead in the dark is alive in the light," it stated.

Christian blinked several times, making sure he was reading it correctly. This was not the first time he'd heard that.

Like a sledgehammer to his brain, a vivid memory came cascading into focus. He was fourteen. Lena was with him in the backyard. A pigeon had died, and Lena wanted to know what to do with it. Natalie came outside with a hammer and nails, thinking they should hang it on the wooden fence to warn other pigeons not to fly near them. Both Christian and Lena appreciated her intentions. However, maybe a bird crucifixion was a little strong. Instead, Christian had begun to dig a grave in the corner of the yard by a large holly tree. He was concentrating so hard on digging out the perfect hole, he never noticed the old man next to him on the other side of the fence. He looked to his left to see both his sisters still with fright.

Christian had whipped his head around, and there stood an Indian. He knew the appropriate term he should use was "Native American." He was rattled but trying not to show it. The man stood no more than six inches from him. The three children stood sweating in the summer heat. The old Indian with leather skin stared at all three. His eyes were terrifyingly large. "There are no birds in the sky above you. I know you have noticed. That dead creature in your hand thought it could outrun the dark. Now you dig its grave. It is too late for all of you."

The children said nothing.

"I am not sorry for the world. The white man built his house on our earth. Now our dead have poisoned his white children. I think it is deserved."

Lena walked closer to the man. "What are you saying, old man?"

The old Indian looked at the dead bird. "Your family and the families before you have been seen. You are judged by my own kin. They have found the three of you worthy. The choice was made for you. You were born into it by your father and his father before him." The man pointed with a long dark fingernail to the ground. "My people lay below your feet. They are dead, but they do not sleep. What is dead in the dark is alive in the light."

Christian Volos stood up from the machine. He felt a daze come over him. His whole life was preceded by tragedy. No emotion of any kind came to him. These memories and photographs gave in to his curious nature. He felt no nostalgia, sympathy, or pain. There was no point in continuing this journey down memory lane.

Christian thanked the librarian for her help on the way out. He was scheduled to be on vacation for the remainder of the week but decided to go into work instead. He figured the night shift guys would enjoy fighting over who got to go home. There was no point in him trying to take the time off. Right now, his head was spinning with memory he didn't want. All he really wanted was to focus on the important work at hand. He needed to visit the herpetology department of the zoo. He had learned over the years that preparation was the key to everything. He needed to gather his resources for the next project.

37

PUZZLE POLITICS

Natalie had not been concerned while being interviewed by police. If anything, it was kind of fun watching them go back and forth trying to put the puzzle together. *How ironic*, she thought. It was the first time she had to talk to the police, and it had nothing to do with her actual crimes. No wonder they had never caught onto her. There was the one detective who seemed sharper than the rest. He was a heavyset man with dark eyes and very intuitive. He had asked her about her family. That was an odd thing to mention. Her family had nothing to do with the occurrence in the hotel. She was struck by a thought on the way back to the city. How did he even know about my family? He'd asked her once they got to the station. She had been riding in the car with him the whole time. There was no way he would have had time to research her. He never asked for names. But he had asked if she had siblings; where she had grown up; and, strangest of all, what middle school had she gone to? Now, it was entirely possible that he had gotten to these questions through plain small talk. The situation was anything but usual. Small talk seemed inappropriate—the middle school question especially. Why did that matter?

Natalie decided to put it out of her mind. It had been a long twenty-four hours, and she needed to lay low until the police stopped contacting her. She was told the district attorney would not pursue a case against her. That was not entirely reassuring. She pondered the thought all the way back to her apartment.

She walked into the cramped one-bedroom and made her way to the shower. She never even unpacked her belongings. She found it more comforting to have everything ready to go, just in case. In case of what? No one suspected her of anything. Was it possible she had been overly cautious all these years? Everything about her was a farce. She wore makeup so that she would never look run-down in front of others. She wore her hair back with large black glasses so that men would not approach her. She bought nice clothes only because that was what young, single attending doctors did. The same went for her apartment. It was littered with "normal" person stuff. People never question someone who has a lot of picture frames in their place. That meant this person has friends and family who love them. It means they are trustworthy, and you as a visitor are safe with them. Any visitors would never even take the time to really look at the photos around her apartment. If they did, they might notice none of the people matched up. There was no continuous cycle of the same faces. If they looked closer, they would see she never took the fake manufactured photos out of the frames. Her apartment had more in common with a Walmart store than it did a family home.

She let the warm water rain down for a while. She saw streaks of dried blood head to the shower drain. The question kept rolling through her mind. "What middle school did you go to?" Why did he ask that? Her and her siblings had all gone to the same school when they were younger. They had grown up in the same area but had moved away years ago. It was not until right now that they would even intentionally try to see each other. They had no connection, no similar friends or jobs, nothing. Then that word hit her like a baseball bat.

They did have a "connection." But it was so widespread, over different places in different times. Things had happened over the course of years. The three of them, no matter how far apart, were killers. Had that detective discovered the similarity? At the end of the day, she and her siblings shared a very distinct connection. It was never spoken of because they never spoke. If one of them became a suspect, it wasn't that far of a jump to the others. They all knew it. They had discretely followed each other's work.

Did he know about all of them? Natalie had learned to trust her gut over the years. Right now, it told her only one thing. The detective knew about Christian. From there, it was nothing more than a deep google search to put the rest in place. If he did not know about Christian, he knew there was a connection of some kind between the dead bodies and one of her siblings. She lay in bed wrestling with decisions to make—or not make.

At 4:00 a.m., she sat up looking into the dark. She would warn them as best she could. She sat up to begin the process of how to warn them. Christian had only used prepaid phones for the last twenty years. He was basically a hermit in a city of four million people. She knew where he worked though. Christian had always preferred animals to humans. Animals acted on instinct, much like Christian. Lena, on the other hand, was a princess in a high castle. In the back of her mind, she had already worked out how this would happen. She would have to act quickly. What she was starting to suspect, meant that detective was already watching for one if not all of them. Strangely enough, the only emotion she did not feel was panic. In fact, she felt calm for the first time in a long time. Natalie rolled back into bed, closed her eyes, and drifted off.

Natalie dreamed now of Maria. Maria was her one and only friend during middle school. Maria was a beautiful girl. Natalie could see clearly Maria's long brunette hair falling over her thin shoulders. She had bright green eyes like large emeralds. Maria sat quietly with Natalie at the lunch table. Maria never needed to speak and was comfortable with silence in the way Natalie was. They were inseparable for a little while. Natalie had felt something deeper for Maria. It was a heat that she wasn't old enough to understand. She only knew that, for the magical little while, she wanted her close.

Natalie stirred in her dreams. Her mind replayed the memory moment to moment. "Maria," she called from her bedroom window. In the darkness of the yard, a figure stood up behind the row of bushes bordering the neighbor's house. Maria ran without making a sound across the yard and under Natalie's bedroom window. Like a female spiderman, she hoisted her light frame on top of the gutter railing. She pulled herself onto the awning and quickly jumped to Natalie's outstretched hands. The two pulled and pushed with all their strength until they both collapsed backward into Natalie's bedroom. On the floor, they laughed at the scene while trying to catch their breath.

Two young girls giggled together atop the covers of a flowery bed. They made jokes about the cheerleaders in school. Maria's hand found its way to Natalie's knee. For several moments, the two got lost looking at each other. Natalie took the risk first. She lifted Maria's hand from her knee, placing a soft kiss on top of it. Maria returned the kindness by pulling her friend into a long kiss on wet lips. The two leaned back, smiling at each other.

Natalie slept now with Maria's arm hugging her stomach. Her sleep was so peaceful, unlike any she had ever known. She blinked her eyes, waking a bit at the cold around her. Her friend's arm was no longer keeping her company. Natalie woke, sitting up in bed and peering into the dark room. She lost her breath. Her heart skipped several beats. Maria was staring at her. The green eyes narrowed in the night. A sparkle caught Natalie from the corner of her eye. The moonlight was glistening off sweat now beaded across Maria's forehead. Maria's breathing was rapid. "There's something standing next to us," she said.

Natalie turned her attention to the end of the bed. In the dark, she saw nothing. She moved her head to the right, seeing now that the moonlight was flooding most of the room. She wasn't looking at darkness. She was looking at a shadow.

Natalie jumped up, now in real time. She couldn't catch her breath from the nightmare. She sobbed softly alone.

38

BE GONE

The encounter at Mida's house had been too overwhelming. Lena couldn't get Mida's face out of her mind. Her husband never even noticed how distracted she had been since returning home. The way her aunt spoke to her, the way she'd looked at her was driving her mad. She kept waiting for a moment of clarity, but it wasn't coming.

Lena decided she needed to clear her head. She had recently joined the CrossFit cult. She had no intention of being one of those scary twentysomething girls. Their abdominal muscles swelled, their faces got rock hard, and their hands started to look like a carpenter's. She was very content where she was physically. At thirty-six, she could still run a six-minute mile and keep up with all the pull-ups. Plus, she could wear a dress and not look like she was preparing for a body-building contest. She went to the factory building that was now a CrossFit sanctuary. She sweated through the hour session of burpees, lunges, and that ridiculous groaning sound from the others.

The only time she made those sounds was when she wanted her husband to think she was enjoying his company.

The workout wrapped up. Lena walked to her locker to grab her stuff. She listened to the silly younger girls give pointers to the desperate soccer moms. It was all so sad. She walked out into the dark, eyeing her car in the distance. She heard the pattern of jogging to her left. The jogger was headed in her direction. Lena wasn't paying it any attention. The pattern of footsteps on the ground grew faster. Lena now felt uncertain. She glanced to her left. It was a masked face under the hood.

"Cops know about Christian," the jogger said and sprinted off into the night.

Two hours later, Lena was still sitting in the parking lot of the CrossFit gym. The car engine was idling quietly. Lena now contemplates her next move. Her sister had taken a great risk to warn her of the impending danger. The initial shock kept her quiet as the jogger took off into the dark buildings. After regaining her composure, Lena wanted to yell for Natalie to come back. She missed her. She missed her brother. Family had always been the three of them, and no one else mattered. Now she took a hard look at reality. It had been only a matter of time before the police came after one of them. She'd noticed those bodies in the news over the years. The names rang out to her from middle school. She was only two years younger than Christian—close enough behind to not know those people in some distant memory. If the cops could pull at one of them, the rest would follow.

Relief took the place of panic. She'd waited all these years to start fresh wherever she wanted. A smile came over her. Her husband would not like the bad news.

He was happy to be home in his apartment. It had been a long night preceded by a long day. Christian usually kept himself awake for forty-eight hours at a time before his body started to fight with him. His calculations right now were that he was at hour fifty-one. Before bedtime, though, he wanted to see his prize catch from the night. Around his shoulder was a dark green Timberland backpack that he had snatched from the lost and found. He could feel the bottom of the bag squirming around. It wasn't the largest one in the cage, not that it needed to be. He had managed to get a female, which are more aggressive. In his closet was an empty glass case. He had kept many creatures in there over the years. Most he had stolen from the zoo. It surprised him that no one had caused a bigger stir over missing creatures known to be extremely dangerous. He felt bad in a way; these creatures could probably smell the many he'd kept in the glass before them.

He turned the backpack upside down, giving it a good shake. Surprisingly, it fell right out into the center of the cage. It remained in a curling position. When outstretched, he knew it was roughly four feet of black death. This mamba would be the deadliest creature he would use yet. It never made him nervous here in the little apartment. Creatures such as this kept good company. He poured a glass of bourbon while admiring the shiny scaling. He could imagine the slow, methodic breathing under camouflage in the jungle—the snake patiently waiting for the prey. He craved that type of freedom. A life spent reacting to survive appealed to him more than anything else. He took a final swig of the brown glory and then decided to call it.

Christian put the lid on the glass enclosure, slipped off his shirt, and went to bed. For a moment, he lay staring at the snake, watching the muscles rise and fall. The rhythm guided him to a peaceful sleep.

39

FLAP, FLAP

Frank had been combing through every file, article, and reference that came up. He had been at it for the last two days, even calling out at work. In front of him was a timeline of homicides dating back to the 1950s. Granted, there was a huge generational gap. From what he could see, there was a spiderweb of death around the family. All the victims from his original cold cases had gone to elementary school together. The oldest brother, Christian, would have been in contact with all of them at some point in those years. He still did not know motive, but he did see the connection. The younger sister had a ring of tragic circumstances befall her patients. Several open medical investigations had occurred while she worked at the hospitals. Frank had gone so far as to call the hospitals and get on the phone with the chief medical officers. He never mentioned her name. But in the time frames, yes, the hospitals had seen a spike in unexplained inpatient deaths. The middle sister was Lena. She was the easiest to follow with her string of unlucky men. Frank decided it was time to meet the older brother in person. Having met Natalie, he was curious how Christian might react.

It was a true fall East Coast day—just the right amount of cold and overcast. It was the kind of day that made it easy to find a watering hole filled with whiskey. Frank, instead, trudged through dead leaves on the side of Gerome Ave. in the west part of the city. He looked ahead at the massive elephant trunk covered in jewels; the sign attached to it read "Philadelphia Zoo." He paid the thirty-five-dollar entrance fee to the nice girl at the ticket counter.

The place was a swarm of kids of all ages. It was easy to pick out the high school groups—everyone acting too cool when deep down they wanted to go crazy over the crocodile pits. The younger kids were more fun to watch. They were excited the way Frank hadn't felt since he was probably their age. Everything was incredible, big, and fun. Frank meandered through the monkey cages. He went to the big cat section. He had forgotten how ferocious tigers looked up close. There was a park ranger doing an educational demonstration next to a rhino. The poor guy had to yell because the roar of the kids was so loud. Frank stood to the side scanning all sides of the park.

He knew after speaking to the park manager that Christian worked the night shift. Those guys came on around seven, right before closing. They had the run of the park all night. Christian was known as a reliable worker. The manager had never had a complaint from him or about him in ten years. He was on the quieter side but friendly during conversations. Frank had used his police influence when he'd called the security supervisor. The man was hesitant at first—until Frank asked about the drug testing policy. The supervisor just wanted the call to be over. He gave Christian up, agreeing to not speak about the inquisition. Overall, it was a positive review of Frank's possible serial murderer.

Currently, it was six forty-five. Frank headed to a sign that read "Security Office." He knew Christian would be stopping in at the start of his shift. Frank hung around pretending to look at the aviary on the opposite side. The color of the birds really grabbed him—so many fluorescent blues, pinks, and oranges flying in circles together as one. Wings of all sizes flapped together, breaking off into a parade for their nests. It was a freeing sight to see. The age-old question of what superpower would you have? Frank's answer was undoubtably the ability to fly.

"It's hypnotizing, isn't it?"

Frank had not even noticed the man next to him. How long had he been standing there looking at birds? He stuttered with a moment of nervousness, "Y-y-yeh it is, I never appreciated them when I was younger."

The man never looked at Frank, only stared straight ahead at the birds. "There is a lot we should've appreciated as children; maybe it would have made us better adults." The man continued, never looking in Frank's direction, "Human beings are a creative mistake. We were supposed to be the better part of the world, but instead, we are its destruction." The man slowly turned toward Frank. "The park is closing soon," he said.

Frank replied, slightly fumbling for his words, "I'm on my way out; just wanted to look at something beautiful first."

The man looked again at the birds. "You found the right thing to look at. Are you here alone?"

Frank hesitated. "Yes. I guess I just needed some time to myself."

The man leaned on the metal pole with his left arm. His

eyes took a long gaze at Frank. "You don't know how alone you are, do you?" With that, the stocky stranger took a last glance toward the birds. His head cocked to the left, taking in a deep breath.

The man walked away in a slow yet strong manner. He went into the security office where he was greeted with, "Hey, there he is!"

Frank felt a chill go down the center of his skull. He couldn't walk away fast enough. His heart didn't settle until he was in his car. He knew now he'd just met Christian Volos. He'd also never felt so insecure in all his life.

40

SHE

The house noticed the recent commotion on the front yard. Someone had come inside, bringing in that fresh air through the front door. The house had not felt such a sensation in several years. A memory of people who had lived within its walls reverberated throughout. In the front yard was a small burnt scar, where one of them had let themselves ablaze. They were forever scorched into the grass. Their ash now lived in the dirt. The other was taken by loud humans with lights and thunderous sirens. Today, years and years later, while the house sat quietly, a familiar human came inside. They were gentle at the doorway, not ramming it open but nudging it kindly. They came in knowing this place. The house knew them as well. It had been a very long time. Many seasons had passed. This human was now bigger than when they left. The house remembered her. She had lived here with the boy so many years before. She, like the boy, had grown. She glided slowly along the walls, just like the man had. She felt the doorways and breathed in deeply all the smells of the house. She went up the stairs; the house was embarrassed at its state of decay. She did not seem to mind. She went room to room, breathing deeper and deeper. She walked, as her brother had walked.

A dark cloud ascends the stairs leading to the basement.

"She is here, Mother."

"Yes, my child."

The cloud passes through the kitchen across the walls into the living room. Over the filth it travels to the bedroom where the woman stands. Now it pauses in midflight behind the woman.

"Where is her brother?"

"He is dead, my child. She walks alone, but she is not lonely."

The woman turns, facing the cloud. Her teeth are bared in a wide grin.

"She looks at us, Mother."

"She is home, my child. She visits her memories in this place."

The woman walks past the cloud returning to the first floor. She exits as quietly as she entered.

The men who built the house should never have poured the concrete. Below the wood and rock and dirt were the bodies. All these years later, the mother and son still rest, entombed forever. The house knew it was cursed. The curse followed these inhabitants forever. It had created monsters in families. Noises came from the children. They held in strange groans. The house knew these sounds because it too made them. It only made them when the wind took off a piece of siding; if a tree branch snapped and fell onto the roof; or if water came in through the basement, choking off the floor. The sounds came from pain. This woman was familiar to the house. She was a reminder of the terrors so many years ago.

41

NUT UP

Frank sat in his garage for several hours. After his encounter with Christian, he was forced to think very hard about how he wanted to pursue this. He had the connection. He had the diagram of murder throughout the entire family. However, he had no actual evidence. Everything he was looking at was conjecture. He knew that all this could be wiped out by a decent lawyer. What did the siblings have in common? The house where they grew up. But that house was left years ago. Would it really supply him with ammo for a case like this? The other question was, Could he bring this to his superiors? He had been around long enough to know they would laugh him right into retirement.

Who was the most prolific killer in the group? Clearly the brother would clear a backlog of cold cases, possibly even more missing person's cases. Frank made the decision he would take Christian himself. Through him, he would get the evidence to investigate the rest of the family. For the first time in who knows how long, he felt fire in his mind again. He was acting as a real detective, hunting true evil. He was flying high like a rookie cop. Alone in a garage, he stared at a scene of macabre.

He stopped for just a moment. He took a breath to really examine what he was looking at. This was not the creation of a small gang of amateur killers. These three had survived the past decade without a hint of suspicion. Here he was, acting like it was a simple matter of knocking on the door to arrest each one of them. They were dangerous in a way he had never seen. They were patient and methodical separately. Each one had his or her own methods. He imagined the chief of police yelling, "Where's the physical evidence?" None of the hospital deaths could be directly related to Natalie other than the fact that she worked there. Lena's lovers had been long dead with no hint of suspicion mentioned in any of it. Assuming she put them all in early graves, plenty of time had passed for her to tidy up any details. His heart sank. What did he have on Christian? He'd gone to school with these people? He made Frank nervous? The only way he could see an end to this was addressing it head-on. If Christian fell, the others might run.

The slight hiccup that could work in his favor was the homicide case that now involved Natalie. A violent death at a hotel, along with multiple hospital fatalities, and only one common denominator. Natalie's connection to these plus Lena's connection to the lovers; add to that Christian's school friends, and just maybe it could work. His theory would at least be enough for an interview session. It would have to do. Frank was prepared to make peace with it if it fell apart.

Two weeks had passed since Natalie's hotel dilemma. She had returned to work as usual. There was a mandatory meeting with hospital administration to assess any psychological trauma she may be having. It was agreed upon that she could return to part-time work with a follow-up assessment in one month. The whole thing had been on the news for a day and then quickly faded. The police had called several times for minute details but nothing more than that.

It depressed her to think she had to lay low for some time as a precautionary measure. She always felt the work she did was the noble thing. These silly, stupid, family members were incapable of making real decisions. The hospitals were too afraid of lawsuits, stepping lightly over every single life-and-death issue. From now until the time was right, she would have to suck up the weak-mindedness of the people around her. She had done what she could for Christian and Lena. In her mind, that was about as much as any one of them could do for the other. She would be ready if the time came. It was not Christian's fault. She hadn't spoken a word to him in years. She knew he had his own reasons for separation. They all fought the demons alone.

42

CUT AND RUN

Lena knew who that running stranger was. She could sense her own blood states away. She would be forever grateful that Natalie had risked what she did to warn her. Lena decided she wouldn't wait around for the dots to be connected. Her whole life, all she ever wanted to know was, What had been haunting them as children? Who had done those terrible things? And she couldn't help but be furious that her parents had allowed it to happen. She realized the old Indian's words were right. She and her siblings had become a scourge on humanity. Without thought, they had all become sociopaths in their own way. The time for reconciling with it was now. She had to forcibly make peace with the fact that she may never get real answers. She packed up the important belongings, with plans to fly to Spain. Once there, if Interpol or anyone came after her, she had no doubt she could disappear into Europe or even Africa. Her simpleton of a husband would be home soon. She needed all the passwords for his accounts and safety security boxes. She didn't want to hurt the man. But certain things were going to happen.

Lena was upstairs in their bedroom when the front door opened. All the WD-40 in the world, and it still had a creak they could never get rid of. "Hello," was his call from the hallway.

How had she ever wound up in a little life like this? She didn't want it anyway, she told herself. "Michael, I need the passwords to all the accounts we have. Also, I need to know if you have anything stashed away."

"Well, hello to you too, honey," he responded.

Suddenly, she hated his fucking polo shirt, his fucking boat shoes, all of it.

He began to walk away from her. "Let's start over, and you ask me how golfing was. Then you tell me what you've made for dinner."

"Michael, what are our account passwords?"

He continued walking away, snickering at her request. Had he taken the time to look at her, he would have noticed the scalpel in her hand. Michael felt the surge of pain rush up his right leg. It was so intense it took the wind out of him. He had never felt something like this. He fell to the ground grabbing at his leg, preparing to howl. He couldn't find his breath; nothing would come out.

A shadow appeared over him, but he couldn't pay it any attention. Blood squirted from the back of his heel, pooling around his foot. He was immediately nauseous, trying to vomit. The shadow above him spoke. "Michael, give me the account passwords."

He didn't recognize the face. It was Lena; he was sure it was Lena. But it wasn't her. This woman had a crooked smile with wide eyes. Her head tilted to the left, glaring at him. Fear and pain gripped him at the same time. He tried to stand; his heel separated further from the rest of his leg. Blood came out in gushes. All he could focus on was the pain.

"I've gone straight through your Achilles. You can still get help and use that leg again. Don't take too long making this decision."

Michael was so confused. He heard muscle and tissue tearing away from his heel. What the hell was happening to his perfect life at this moment? He fumbled for words, eventually finding them, "In my phone under notes, I have all the important ones." Tears began pouring down his cheeks. "Why the fuck did you do this? Fuck you, fuck you, bitch."

Lena looked at him, feeling the smallest amount of pity. "It's not fair that things have been so easy for you. I think it's only fair that you suffer to repay the universe for its kindness." With that, she swiped fast with her right hand.

Michael saw the movement. He followed her hand but couldn't block it because he was gripping his injured leg. He felt warmth dripping down the front of his pink polo. His neck was suddenly wet. He held it with the palm of his left hand.

Things began to get blurry; he felt air from his chest. Every time he took a breath, it was smaller and smaller. Panic set into his face. He looked down at the blood now covering his shirt, making its way onto his cargo shorts. *This is going to stain*, he thought before closing his eyes.

He took his last breath as Lena headed out the door. She had what she needed. With any luck, the police wouldn't put it all together for a few days. By then, she would be a ghost.

43

GOODBYES

Christian felt a wave of relief standing in his apartment. It felt good to have the next project in mind. He had already scoped out Jared's work schedule. His plan was to take him tomorrow night. Christian stood alone in the quiet. He closed his eyes, daydreaming about the pain that would soon come to someone so deserving. A knock sounded on the door. It startled him but did not completely throw him off guard. Christian went to his corner closet. In the back, he kept a prized possession from his teenage years. It was a three-foot steel machete. It had a serrated edge that he had used on more than one occasion to remove someone from their own limb. He went to the door, not sure what to expect.

Frank stood at the doorway. He had finally gotten the security supervisor to give up Christian Volos's home address, only after the threat of a court order. Frank knew the chance of that was slim, but the supervisor didn't know that. The address shocked him. It was a two-story walk-up on Diamond

Street. The locals referred to it as D Block. Frank had stopped to ask some neighbor on the porch stoop if they knew Christian. Their answers were short and evasive. He couldn't tell if they were being loyal or fearful. On a normal occasion, a thirtysomething-year-old single guy living alone on this block would definitely stand out. This particular section of North Philadelphia was known to be a shady region even by Philadelphia standards. It began just north of the art museum area and ran for miles along Broad Street. A lot of cities in the United States could talk about rough areas, ghettos, and so on. This section of one of the oldest cities in the country was the land that time had forgotten. A person could drive two miles down any block and not see a single operating business. Every other home was either vacant or condemned. Brick from falling buildings littered the sidewalks. The residents had been forgotten about by the city housing authority. For many years, the community had tried bringing money into the region. The city felt it was a waste of funds because there were no tourist attractions of any kind. It was also a landlocked region. Other parts of the city had been reinvigorated to build waterfront attractions. The north had been left to rot by officials.

Before Frank stepped into the doorway, he took a long look at his alien surroundings. If something went wrong in this situation, he had no doubt that no one would hear about it. It occurred to him that this could be the last time he was seen by anyone. Frank quietly climbed the wooden stairs up. The apartment had a number 4 painted in black on the door. He knocked twice while trying to slow his heart rate.

Light footsteps came from inside. A shirtless, barefoot Christian answered. He wore only a pair of ratty jeans. He stared at Frank. An eternity passed between them in silence. Before Frank could speak, Christian said to him, "I know you."

Frank responded, "Mr. Volos, we met—"

Christian cut him off, never changing his gaze or speech pattern, "I have always known you. You have spent years making your way here. I hope you're not disappointed. Did you bring any friends?" Christian looked past Frank, tilting his head over Frank's shoulder. He smiled at him. "No?" "Well that's OK. More will come eventually."

Frank began again. "Mr. Volos, I am Detective Frank—"

Christian cut him off again, "Do you remember what you told me the first time we met?"

Frank thought for a moment. "I told you I wanted to look at something beautiful."

"That's right," Christian said. "Now I am going to look at something beautiful." With that, Christian opened the door completely.

Frank could see right away there was a large glass case behind him in the middle of what appeared to be a small studio apartment. Christian brought his left arm up at his side. Frank saw the shiny weapon raised. Christian swung backward, away from Frank. The huge blade smashed into the glass case, shattering it. Frank saw something stir in the case. Without thinking, he pulled his issued 9mm from his hip holster. He pointed it at Christian's forehead. Behind him, something was moving. Frank was unsure what he was looking at. It was black and hissing. It fell to the ground behind Christian's feet.

"Goodbye, Detective." With that, Christian slammed the door shut.

Frank stood with his gun raised, wondering what in the hell he had just witnessed.

Inside the apartment, Christian stood alone listening to the movement behind him. He took a wide stride into the kitchen area, not bothering to avoid walking through the glass scattered across the apartment floor. On the counter sat the bottle of bourbon. After his projects, Christian liked to have a drink alone. He put the machete down on the counter. The hissing continued behind him. He unbuttoned his jeans and pulled them off. He grabbed the bottle by the neck. He turned and sat down directly into the glass shards. Now he sat, naked on the floor. His legs were spread out as he sipped from the bottle.

The movement made its way closer to him. Christian could see the snake. Its head darted quickly side to side. "You are beautiful," he said, taking a long pull from the bottle. The snake is now inches from him. "Come get it, motherfucker," Christian said as the mamba bit down into his unprotected calf.

There are several people within a hospital who are considered the most senior or administrative. Three of them were now standing with Natalie in an otherwise empty conference room—the chief nursing officer, a tightly wound seventy-year-old woman; the chief medical officer, a sixty-five-year-old critical care doctor who everyone knew as "Dr. Chuck"; and the hospital CEO, Alex Cortez Esquire. These three people oversaw the day-to-day operations of a major hospital network in the City of Brotherly Love. Ten minutes ago, Natalie had been doing her rounds with the residents in the ICU. She had been approached by all three and asked to come with them.

Nancy, the uptight CNO, had done most of the talking. "We have been contacted by law enforcement as to the strange deaths of several patients. We have contacted human resources as well, who should be here soon. The police department asked that we take you off the floor so that they may speak to you privately. There is also some news about your brother. The police would like to discuss that as well."

Natalie looked at all three, offering no facial response. She had waited several minutes, making it very uncomfortable in the room. Finally, she looked at each one individually, taking her time to scan their uncomfortableness. "Fuck it," was all she said. With that, she blew past the three administrators and out of the conference room.

Down the hall, she could see the unit secretary directing a large hoard of men with badges in her direction. The men saw her immediately and quickened their pace. The detective was out in front. Natalie had fractions of a second. Her decision was made that quickly. She cut left into the nearest ICU room. To the right, Natalie saw a patient, who, fortunately, was not conscious. The patient was an elderly man on a ventilator with a tube down his throat. *Good*, she thought.

She had closed the sliding glass door behind her. She unlocked the patient's bed, along with the IV pump and vent. With a few quick movements, she pushed the patient with all the attachments directly in front of the door. The group of cops and clinicians arrived, only to find they had to be careful or risk injuring the sedated patient.

Natalie went to the window overlooking downtown Philadelphia. "It really is a nice view," she whispered to herself. Natalie reached under the hospital bed for the oxygen tank. She knew every bed had to have one for transportation. She swung the large green tank at the window, blowing it open. Cold air blasted in from the twenty floors below. At the base of the window was a line of rigid glass, still sitting in the molding.

Natalie could hear the frantic voices in the background. She heard the wheels of the bed move. "Open the door! Open the door!" They would be on her soon.

She took in the view for one more second. In the corner of her eye came the strangest sight. A large black crow flew in small circles outside the window. It stopped long enough to look Natalie in the eyes. A long exhale streamed out of her nose. Calm now rose in her bones. With force, she let her neck down onto the glass, simultaneously letting her legs give way. Her last sensation was the glass cutting clear across her neck and hitting her spine. Blood spurts in every direction.

The door behind her was opened. Natalie's eyes dilated; she was gone.

Frank had just returned from the catastrophe at the hospital. He'd specifically told the administrators not to interfere in any way. Two of the siblings were now dead. This had turned into a bloodbath projected over every single news cycle on the planet. Bringing the evidence to his commanding officer and district attorney was one thing. They had been completely receptive, mostly because it had the potential to solve so many cold cases. He was mad at himself for waiting. The search warrant for Christian's apartment had gone through the judge in record time. He had brought a full SWAT unit, which was probably what he should have done in the first place. What they found was enough to disturb even seasoned veterans on the force. They knocked the door down to find a horror show on the floor. The thirty-seven-year old was naked, sitting spread-eagle on a floor of glass. He was covered in small bites. The most disturbing part was the black coil sleeping comfortably on his head.

Frank's main concern now was finding the other sister. The unit he'd sent to her house had reported a homicide. Frank had been at the hospital trying to plug the laceration across Natalie Volos's throat when the call had come over his radio. Lena Volos had slaughtered her husband before running. His superiors agreed on a nationwide all-points bulletin, or APB. He tried to consider her mental state. The other two had been loners. They were clearly afraid of being caught, viewing suicide as the way out. He did not want that for Lena. It was never a good thing to finish a case with a death. However, she had proven herself to be violent and an obvious sociopath.

There was a call from Bank of America. They had received notification of the APB. Lena had just left the bank after withdrawing from all her accounts. The bank manager informed them she had been outraged to learn her husband's safety deposit box was not at that branch. She would have to go to the Market Street branch next to city hall.

Lena parked around the corner near the 7-Eleven. She was planning on not spending any more time than necessary. With any luck, they would not look at her maiden name. The news had listed her siblings under Volos. She had not used that name in fifteen years. She covered her face with a silk scarf given to her by husband number two.

As she walked toward the building, a sound shook her eardrums. *Caw! Caw!* It came from behind her. For a second in time, Lena stared at the two crows seated on the drainpipe coming off the side of the building. The birds made no movement. They only looked at Lena. On she went.

Lena entered the bank. Immediate tension came from the portly security guard standing inside the security door by the way he turned his body. She walked past a row of ATMs, none of which were in use. She didn't feel nervous until the manager came walking out to meet her. At that moment, she knew this had been a mistake.

She had been greedy her whole life. She knew it. Yet she couldn't let that spoiled bitch of a husband leave this world without knowing she was going to take everything. She could feel the presence of a security guard over her shoulder. She was boxed in. The manager stood in front of her, attempting to make pleasantries. Another security guard had just flanked her from the right. The manager's words came out as distant garble.

Fuck you all, she thought.

Lena could hear the speeding and then slowing of cars out front. Footsteps came alive by the hundreds it seemed. She could feel everything, fast breath in the air, vibration in the ground; she made her decision. Lena dropped her purse from her right shoulder. In her hand was the same blade she had used on her husband. "Sorry for this," was all she spouted as she stepped forward and put the knife straight into the bank manager's left eye.

The world went still for a moment. She saw the manager scream with a mouth wide open. The sound erupted along with an explosion. She felt a deep cool breeze as she stumbled forward. With her last look, she saw the back of her head splatter across the manager's shirt. Then there was nothing.

44

DRY YOUR EYES

There was no way to control the news cycle. The story of so many unsolved, mysterious murders captivated the country. The first recorded family of murderers with little to no connection as adults. One sibling's murders had nothing to do with the other. The psychological studies would continue on for generations. Today was not about the events. Frank decided to attend the lonely memorial at Wilbert Cemetery. The day itself was enough to depress anyone. The wind brought cold from all directions, along with rain that no umbrella could block out completely. Christian's body had been cremated after the investigation. Natalie had been an organ donor, and so, in the end, she wound up doing some actual good.

This memorial was for Lena. Only three other people stood in the dark weather by a lonely headstone. There was a reverend, not reading from the Bible but instead philosophizing on what could have been a productive life. Next to him was a tall, lean woman. She had sharp features that seemed pale next to her black dress. The person who caught his eye was standing about twenty yards beyond the grave. The man wore a tuxedo shrouded across the shoulders with silver braided hair. He held on to a wooden cane that glittered with rain droplets bouncing off it. He stared directly at Frank. Frank was transfixed by the dark eyes of this man. He heard words in the background but couldn't look away from this stalker.

The old man's free hand came up to his mouth. Using a brown leathery index finger, he pointed at the tall woman in black. Frank glanced at her to see she was staring right back at him. His pulse doubled in his chest. Frank's eyes quickly darted back to the Native American. The leathery man smiled ear to ear at him.

The reverend spoke for about ten minutes before finishing up. Frank turned to walk away, feeling nerves in his gut from the uncomfortable scene. His eyes looked upward, and there in the trees was a collection of black crows staring back at him. In the center of the crows sat a haze. Frank tried to fix his eyes. He was sure of what he was seeing. A cloud of darkness sat in the center of an army of crows. Nothing moved. Everything looked at him. Sound stood still. He felt a familiar feeling, like the one he'd gotten the first time he had met Christian while staring at the beautiful birds.

A hand landed on his shoulder. He was startled, grateful for the distraction. The tall woman stood next to him, looking up at the audience. She spoke without turning in his direction. "I am Mida," she said. "They were my nieces and nephew."

Frank looked at her. "I am sorry about how this played out."

Her hand slid off his shoulder. Her head turned toward him. The aunt's eyes grew wide—so bright he swore they turned yellow. Her mouth contorted with a thin smile. He had only seen one other person make that same face. The aunt's nose went up.

"What is it?" Frank asked.

A low, sharp voice came out that froze his bones in place. "You smell funny," she replied.